CHIMERA CATALYST

Book One of the Finder Series

By
Susan Kuchinskas

www.pandamoonpublishing.com

Jacket design and illustrations © Pandamoon Publishing

Art Direction by Don Kramer: Pandamoon Publishing
Editing by Zara Kramer, Rachel Schoenbauer, Josephine Hao, and Jessica Reino: Pandamoon Publishing

Pandamoon Publishing and the portrayal of a panda and a moon are registered trademarks of Pandamoon Publishing.

Library of Congress Cataloging-in-Publication Data is on file at the Library of Congress, Washington, D.C.

Edition: 1, Version 1.00
ISBN-13: 978-1-945502-80-4

DEDICATION

To all the creatures, human and otherwise,
who've taught me how to be free.

CHIMERA CATALYST

PROLOGUE

I can't clear the brush fast enough. These things can't stop growing. I cut one branch and three more spring out from the cut. I'm trying to clear a nice desert here, but the damned shrubs shrub faster than I can cut them down.

I send the Parrot out on a reconnaissance mission. Is there any end to this goddamned shrubbery? I watch the blue flash of his back take off into the orange sky. I watch the blue dwindle until it's subsumed and the sky is all orange again. I stop cutting brush and just wait. The Parrot will find out. There may be no point to going on.

Then I see the blue flash undwindling, growing back into parrot again. He swoops down and plants all four feet, trying to skid to a stop, plowing up a mound of dust that does little to brake him. In fact, it's only one of the fucking shrubs that finally brings him to a halt.

I can see it in his eyes—and it's not good. There's a lot of shrub out there, a lot of shrubs and a lot of dust.

It would be different if it was just the Parrot—if I wasn't there. He knows that. I can see that in his eyes, too. He'd fly over all this brush and not stop until he reached the top of that mountain. And maybe there'd be something to eat up there. Me, all I can do is trudge. Trudge and cut brush.

But the Parrot won't leave me. I don't have to look into his eyes to know that. There can be a weird bond between two different animals, and we're three animals between us. Parrots mate for life, and that's a long life. Longer than humans, if the human is careless with himself. The dog in him is as loyal as a parrot. And me, I'm as much a victim of that bond as he is. I love the Parrot.

That means cutting down the shrubs even though there's little hope that they'll stop growing long enough for me to make a trail. It's going to be a long day.

Here's how I made the Parrot. I bought several lines of wild-type avian ORF clones from a junk DNA shop. I thawed out a couple grams of Benson's DNA that I'd stashed in the freezer after she'd died. She was the best dog I'd ever had, smart as a person but still with that canine lust for life.

I went at all the DNA strings with CRISPR, snipping out sections of the genetic code from the canine and bird gene sequences. Then, I used the CRISPR tool to combine bird sequences with dog sequences into one coherent string. I spliced and diced and eventually found a couple of sequences that might have almost made sense. Then, I opened three parrot eggs that I got off my friend at the underground animal market, and carefully teased the germinal discs away from the yolk and albumen. Next, I cut out some of the gene sequences in each one, fitting in my mutant DNA. That's where the magic happens.

I did one last thing. I inserted my own neuroplastin-coding gene. It probably wouldn't be expressed, but part of me would be in him.

I nudged the germinal discs back in place, nestled between yolk and albumen, and closed the shells with bioethylene plastic. I cradled the eggs in a padded, sterilized rack and put the rack into the incubator at 99.5 degrees Fahrenheit—parrot temp—and ignored it for three weeks. Then, I began monitoring the eggs with infrared sensors. Two of them were nonviable, but the third had a strong and steady heartbeat. I needed to tweak the temperature a few times, and it took a dog's full nine weeks for the embryo to mature. At the right time, I had to break the shell.

He was the most beautiful thing I'd ever seen, even newly hatched. Weighing just eight ounces, he'd eventually grow to the size of a small parrot. His four little paws ended in yellow claws with toenails no thicker than an eyelash. His wings were just stubs, but already, there was a faint blaze of blue fur down his back.

I fed him the same things I ate, ground up in a blender, with an extra dose of vitamin D and calcium to make his bones strong. I kept him next to me, carrying him in an extra t-shirt tied around my shoulder like a sling. That's when the bond began, for both of us.

Here's why I made him: because I could. Because I wanted to. Because I needed something outside of myself that could press back against me and hold my insides in.

Those are the poetic reasons, the things I like to tell myself. There's another reason that's not so poetic.

I need the Parrot to do my job.

I find things, usually things that don't want to be found. Not digital things—there are plenty of screen jockeys who can do that. I take on the old-fashioned work of finding things in the physical world—and, for more money, sometimes I'll bring them back. Usually, it's something that doesn't want to be brought back.

It suits me to work like this. I came up the hard way. My father worked in one of the last big supermarkets, but he died in a flu pandemic when I was seven. My mother went to work as a maid for some rich 1-percenter. This was right around the time of the Big Change, when the weather got screwed up for good, when New Orleans and Seattle went underwater, and the California deserts moved west.

With my mother gone all day, I stopped going to school and lived in the worlds of multiplayer games. When that got old, I started reading forums on the internet. Then, I started tinkering. I sold digital, in-world goods to buy my first basic kits and chemicals. I was good at hacking and cracking, and good at the biologics.

I'm good at finding, too.

But it's always good to have another pair of eyes, even better when they're attached to something small and strong that can travel far distances, rising above obstacles in its path. Something with dogged determination. That's good, too.

The Parrot is a finding machine. Something about the mix of dog and bird created something much greater than its parts. He can see a raisin stuck to the side of a tree 3,000 yards away. He can smell a speck of shit stuck to a shoe in the next county. Or, as in this case, he can unspool the unique pheromones of one woman from the city stink we came from.

The woman is named Miraluna Rose.

She's a woman worth finding.

CHAPTER 1
4.7 days earlier

Here's how we got stuck in this brush.

I was in my workshop, fiddling with a little chimera I was making—just a hobby thing. A brine shrimp with a touch of lemur, enough to make its little legs able to grasp. I was thinking Sea Monkey, something I saw in an antique comic book. The door sensor ponged, and the camera showed two men dressed in black. Behind them, an Uber shut its doors and buzzed off down the street. The Parrot looked up from his bed on top of the entertainment system, watching me to see if his play should be bird or dog. I gave him a nod: bird is the play. This is some business.

I opened the door and confirmed that my camera impression was on the money. The thin one was weak but rich. The thick one was the thin one's muscle, but not stupid. This wasn't the first time strangers had shown up at my door, and there's only one reason they want to stay off the media grid and talk in person. They want to find something illegal. That's okay with me, there's more money in contraband than in the simply lost. People are always ready to pay more to get something they shouldn't have.

"Come in and sit down," I told them. I never play games with them, pretending I don't know why they're here. They sat down on the leather sofa and I sat back down on my bench chair. The Parrot flew to my shoulder and settled himself against my neck, snuffling my hair. Thin Man winced a little. "Why don't you tell me what you're looking for?"

"You're the Finder, right?"

"Right." I'm always patient with them, too.

Thick Man took out a mobile and scanned the room. Thin Man glanced at him and he nodded.

Now I was offended. "Yes, this room is secure." I glanced at my water recycler. It was a third full. "Can I offer you both some water?" I asked politely, but I meant it as an insult. Clearly, these men could drink water whenever they wanted.

"Thank you, we're fine," Thin Man said. Of course, he would be—always. Him and Thick Man, too.

"So, do you want to tell me why you're here?"

At another nod from Thin Man, Thick Man swiped the mobile and aimed the screen toward me. I slipped on a latex glove and reached for it. Now, it was Thin Man who looked offended. I shrugged and pondered the image on the screen.

I could immediately tell she was beautiful, in all the normal ways—hair, eyes, mouth, neck—the photo didn't show her torso but I imagined the lush curve of her shoulders extending down to frame an upmarket body. Beautiful like that means nothing to me, although I could see the appeal for a rich wanker like Thin Man. I zoomed in a little and saw what the beauty hid from a careless glance.

She made me feel like a lost cat prowling in a driving rainstorm searching for the thin thread of scent that would draw me home to light and warmth and caress. Her face made me realize that everything I'd ever craved was unworthy. Her lips told me I'd never known soft. I wanted her. And that wanting spooked me. I don't like to want things. Wanting is weakness.

Thin Man had watched these things move across my face. He nodded. "Exactly."

I handed the device back and slid the glove off inside out, tossed it into the organic recycling. Then I reached up to bury my fingers in the feathers of the Parrot's chest.

"Tell me."

"Her name is Miraluna Rose. She was kidnapped from my home last night."

"Is she your daughter?" I knew she wasn't.

He got stiff; I could see the pissy he was trying to stifle. "No."

"Wife? Girlfriend?" He shook his head. "Live-in maid?"

"She's my legal mate—if it matters."

I shrugged. "What do the police say?"

He sneered. "I don't want to use the police. I'd prefer to handle this privately and quickly, without having to deal with the bureaucracy."

This wasn't so unusual. Pretty much everything has been privatized these days for those who can afford it, even handling crime. If this *was* a crime. I wasn't so sure; there was something off about the connection between this lump of moneyed charm and the woman in the photo who carried a charge like an IED.

"If I take the job," I told him, "I'll need access to her profile—and yours."

He nodded, but with as much disgust as if I'd asked to sniff his butt. "Now?"

"Why not?" I picked up my own mobile and held it out. He drew his from his pocket—a sleek, paper-thin model with a titanium case—and beamed to mine. "And I'll need a copy of her picture—Miraluna Rose—any other photos or videos you have, and all her accounts. Do you have her passwords?"

He made the butt-sniff face again. "No."

"That just makes it a little more expensive. Give me what you have. Oh, and I also need the login for the cloud where your security camera footage is stored."

"Then I'm going to need a nondisclosure agreement from you."

"It's not necessary, but if a non-D will make you feel better..."

At a nod from his boss, Thick Man took out his mobile again, swiped and touched a few times, then pointed it toward mine. When the light went off, I put mine back on the desk; my mom taught me it's rude to check out someone's beam while they're watching.

"And I'll need fifteen coins. Fifteen today and fifteen every day until I find her."

Now we were back in his comfort zone. "Send me a one-way key to your wallet and I'll make the transfer today."

"I'll be in touch."

Thick Man swiped his mobile a few times and it responded with a *burble* to let them know an Uber was pulling up. I palmed the interior lock, let them out into the haze of the street, then locked up behind them. I was already thinking about the woman.

* * *

I went to my big screen and logged into Thin Man's public profile. His social name was BruceWayne. Cute. He'd have had to pay some ID squatter plenty to get such a top-level social name. As I'd expected, he was in the 1 percent; on the boards of a few of the obvious rich-guy companies—biotech, space tourism, drone deliveries. All the accoutrements of the elite. A house in the clean, grassless hills of Grass Valley, far enough from the urban sprawl for comfort but close enough to jet to Silicon Valley for those high-powered board meetings. I could have found his official identity easy enough; I've got the APIs for the backdoors in Google, Whatsapp, SZiz and the rest. But I was itching to see his surveillance footage.

The Parrot gave a little *yip*. He gets bored. I handed him a dog biscuit. The dog in him makes him easy.

I tried to tell myself I was interested in the case, and the home security footage could be telling. Even I didn't buy it. I wanted to see her. I shut the feeling up in the back of my mind.

His home security setup was pretty standard: coverage of every exterior door and window; wide-angle cameras providing a 360-view of the gravel lawn sloping down to high walls with a single iron gate; and one inside camera aimed to show anyone who came to the door.

I wasn't buying this, either. I'd bet real money he watched her. How could he not?

I dug around and found it hidden in with his provider's boilerplate files, disguised as an FAQ. The file opened to a view of a bedroom. Of course. His spy camera. The camera showed a room like the inside of a tropical flower. The walls were covered in a giant, orange paisley print. Silky fuchsia drapes billowed onto a shaggy white carpet. The bed, with a fluffy coverlet patterned in fuchsia, orange, purple and green, rested in what looked like an abstraction of a seashell—smooth, curvy, and opalescent white.

I hit the back arrow until I saw a flash of movement, then slid the knob back more slowly. And there she was. The time stamp was 10:32 p.m. She came out of the bathroom door wearing a black slip. Did women still wear slips? Her hair, which was dyed sea green, was loose around her face and down her back like a tumble of seaweed. A jade green tattoo peeked out from her mane of hair and made its way down her spine, disappearing into the low back of her slip. She went to a bureau and looped several strands of beads around her neck, stepped into stiletto-heeled boots. Not a slip, a dress. A very small, thin dress. She looked in the mirror, picked up a purse, and left, closing the door behind her. No kidnapping worries for her.

I backed up again and held it on the moment when she looked at herself. I zoomed in. As the image got bigger, the pretty girl getting ready to go out and be admired resolved into a woman who wore the pretty girl like a dress. This woman had the long muscles of a cat sleeked over with a thin layer of baby fat. Her face in profile showed a slightly snub nose and lips turned up at the corners in a subtle, permanent smile. She looked like she owned herself.

My next step was picking up the video from the camera in the entry, tracing her path out the door, down the driveway and then picking up the trail again from the public security cameras. But that could wait. I left her up there, frozen in a moment when she was all beauty and intention.

The Parrot *greeped* softly. It was time for our bedtime snack.

CHAPTER 2

Morning dawned for me, as it usually did, around noon. The Parrot was scratching around at the foot of the bed like he expected to find some nice, tasty worms there. It's his subtle way of letting me know he wants to be fed. It took me a while to get going, as it usually did. In the evenings, after the deprenyl and PEA have peaked, I start my relaxation and sleep stack—phenibut, picamilon and L-theanine with some CBD drops. I goose them with a little progesterone. Call me crazy, but it works for me. It makes for a gentle swoop down into sleep. But the PEA and the phenibut fight with each other a little, and that leaves me with quite a bit of brain fog in the morning—but only until I inject the testosterone and drop the Nootropil. Then I'm good to go.

Once I pepped back up, I took the Parrot up on the roof. His turds are something. They won't go through the recycler, I found out the hard way. While he pooped, I looked out over Berkeley. To the north and east, the University of California covered the hills as far as I could see. Chez Panisse Tower almost blocked my view of the edge of the Black Zone that used to be Lawrence Berkeley Lab. The streets were thick with Googles heading west, the little autonomous pods herding themselves in a solid stream toward the Transbay Tube. In the other direction, driverless Ubers, Bizibikes, and platoons of Bridj vans flowed toward downtown and UC. I watched one lone, defiant jogger halting the pods as she moved north along Shattuck, her progress looking like a ripple in the flow of vehicles.

I kept stealing sidelong glances at the big screen as I made me and the Parrot breakfast. Shredded seaweed, pickled radishes, and cricket flakes over brown rice imported from Antarctica. The rice was pricey but made all the difference.

Then I got down to work. I brought up the surveillance footage of the entryway and picked a point in time two minutes before Miraluna Rose walked out her bedroom door. The scene was as still as a photograph. No Miraluna Rose leaving for a party.

To be certain, I backed up until 9:30 p.m. and then watched until five minutes after my time stamp. Nothing moved. I worked systematically around the exterior camera footage. The house was a grand, old stucco two-story from the 1920s in a vaguely Spanish style. Its windows had been replaced with Hyper Glass that carefully mimicked traditional glass, so they didn't spoil the illusion of old money. In the back, the former swimming pool had been stylishly landscaped to create a small canyon of colored rock to which exotic succulents clung. The gravel in the side yards was meticulously groomed, raked into elaborate patterns. I got excited by a flash of movement near the southeast corner of the building but it turned out to be a lizard.

I went back to the entryway footage and fast-forwarded until I saw the next flicker of movement. It was Thin Man, coming in the door at 8:09 a.m. yesterday morning, the morning after Miraluna Rose had supposedly disappeared. He was wearing the kind of garb rich assholes wear to get exercise, and his silver hair was damp with sweat or, more likely, a luxurious shower.

One hour and thirty-seven minutes later, Thick Man opened the door and entered. Thin Man had found her missing. After that, lots of men came and went, all with the groomed and bulky look of private security loaded with technology.

Miraluna Rose had left her bedroom and vanished without leaving a video trace.

* * *

But everyone leaves traces somewhere. Thin Man had given me sub-admin access to her profiles. I could look at whatever I wanted, just not add or subtract anything. She'd been missing some forty-eight hours. I slurped all her data for the past seven days into an analytics platform I like. It's designed for advertising, but it can do some freaky stuff if you run custom reports.

The data showed that she'd spent the two days before she'd vanished moving around residential and shopping districts in Laxangeles. She'd bought a fair amount of the usual downloads and streams, as well as the kind of physical goods you'd expect an affluent young woman to acquire. The only interesting thing was the end of her GPS trail. It ended at 3:14 p.m. on the day of her disappearance at the Beverly Center. I sighed. It was obviously a spoof, but I'd have to check it out.

I pulled the coordinates of every location where she'd stopped more than ten minutes and sent the map to my mobile. As long as I had to leave the warehouse, I might as well play finder the old-fashioned way.

The Parrot alerted when I picked up my fob. "Sorry, buddy," I told him. "This is person shit I gotta do." Chimeras aren't exactly illegal but they attract a lot of attention from the freaks and nuts. I just didn't want to deal with it today. It was too hot.

I put some meal worms in his dish to console him. The bird in him would have disdained this peace offering, but the dog went for it.

CHAPTER 3

I took the bullet train down to Laxangeles, crunching data as I rode. Coordinates 34.075039° N, 118.377026° W turned out to be in the linens department at Nordstrom. I found the spoofing transmitter tucked away under a stack of 500-thread-count bamboo sheets in olive green. It was the size of my thumbnail and the generic black plastic of old-school electronics. I took a photo and zoomed in until I saw the rough patch where the make and model number had been scraped off. It was the kind of transmitter you could buy from spy shops all over the internet, but scratching off the identification was a good touch. It confirmed what I had already gleaned from the fact that Miraluna Rose had gone home and gotten ready for a nice night out after her GPS trail ended. She hadn't been kidnapped. She'd run away.

I parked myself in a falafel shop on the wrong side of Beverly to plan my next move. A couple of gearheads eyed me through their headsets and then went back to their augmented reality dreams. I looked at the map of her travels over that day and the one before. Nothing jumped out. I decided to follow up on her personal contacts. I sorted my list of her locations by dwell time and then ran a quick address lookup on Streetly. Two mornings ago, at 11:01 a.m., she'd spent close to an hour at a house on Mulholland Drive. I moshed the global newsfeed with semantic analysis of social media and found it was owned by someone named RealReal. I took the time to dig for his official identity. Aman Nihelroush. Images showed a man who could be thirties to a very well-cared-for fifty, with cinnamon skin, a swimmer's body, and the kind of messy hair that takes plenty of primping to get right. I accessed his social graph and created an on-the-fly persona that had just the right amount of overlap via second- and third-degree contacts. Nihelroush was in real estate, so my persona was an angel investor looking to get into something more tangible than friends-and-family shares. I based this false persona in Toronto, to add some urgency to a meeting request, and named him Thad Sayers, a bland and un-alarming ID with a scent of money to it. Then I added the new persona to his contacts. That's a nice little trick I learned in one of my previous employments.

I pinged him a meeting request. F2F. He wouldn't remember any Thad Sayers, but he'd believe his contact list. Then, while I waited for a response, I began sorting through Miraluna Rose's other stopping points. There was another residence in Hollywood that looked interesting, and oddly, the Seattle Public Library. I hacked into the library's records, looking for an anonymized user that might match up to my quarry. Yes, I had started thinking of her as quarry.

It was slow going and a waste of time. No one reads actual books anymore, and you don't have to go to the physical library to check out content. Most libraries are really just preserved as a glorious place for bums to hang out. If Miraluna Rose had spent 23.2 minutes there, it wasn't to do any reading. Still, you never know what may be part of a pattern, so you have to look at it all.

I was still trolling through the user files when my mobile chimed. Nihelroush had messaged me.

Thad. Hope you're well

You, too. Long time

Indeed. Checkit

I'm in LA. Want to meet up? I'm down here doing deals. Can't say ovr txt

Frazzed. Want to come by? I'm home

Sounds good txt me your address

Here it comes. Whats your ETA

20?

CU

* * *

I Ubered myself up the mountain, following Mulholland as it snaked past the charred ruins of a recent flash fire and up into the hardpan where designer mansions gripped the barren hills. At least they still had a view.

The house was a pretentious, architected-to-death concrete fortress, clearly designed after the Big Change, with small, recessed Hyper Glass windows to keep out the heat. I held my palm up to the door's reader so it could scan my prints. No, I hadn't forgotten to attach my real prints to Thad Sayer's bogus profile. It's the simplest way to do it, and no door hardware is smart enough to do a cross-match of the entire citizen database.

The door opened onto a room like a still pond in northern woods. A glossy gray concrete floor seemed to spill out a wall of windows on its far side to mix with the gray haze of Laxangeles spread out below. Pods of glossy furniture rose from its surface like mushrooms. Nihelroush loomed out of the gloom to stand the polite four feet away. He was medium height, with the kind of skinnyness that is very strong. He was wearing a sort of hipster's version of a kurta woven with gray-on-gray checks that made me jealous; he looked cool and seemed to float on the surface of the floor. His hair lay smooth and soft back from his brow. Maybe he'd run out of hair gel.

"Dude."

"Dude." The polite old forms are important to guys like this.

"Care for some water?"

"Thanks."

"I've got an interesting bottle from Ireland."

Of course. It's guys like him who destroyed the polar ice, so now, let's chug it down. I sat on a low couch upholstered in hologram plastic patterned with leaves to fit into the woodland theme. Even though the very rich have the very best in decontamination services, the surfaces in their public rooms tend toward the wipeable.

Nihelroush padded back with a tray and two glasses of water. My hand embraced the chill as I took mine, reminding myself not to gulp it. He held up his glass for a salute.

"Cheers," I said and took a sip. It tasted just like water. Nice clean water that maybe hadn't been through anyone's kidneys in the last forty-eight hours.

"So, Thad, you're here doing deals. How can I help you?"

I settled my back against the cool plastic, cradling my water against my chest. "It's one particular deal. Miraluna Rose."

If the Parrot had been on my shoulder, I would have felt his claws dig in a little. But I didn't need him to tell me the geist in the room had gotten tense.

"Who?"

I sold him a little time. "Miraluna Rose. The protégée of BruceWayne. Dyes her hair green to match her eyes? She went missing two days ago."

"Ahh, the beautiful, green-haired girl. Yes, I've met her a few times. Why do you think I can help you?"

"You run in the same circles. Rich. Powerful. Partying. Maybe you noticed something. Someone with her who didn't seem to belong."

His eyes narrowed. "Look, Thad. Business is business. You said you were looking for deals. Now, you're fishing for information about a woman. Excuse me, but you're wasting my time." He pointedly swiped his smartwatch.

"She was here yesterday. Why?"

He stood up. "You're not one of my contacts. Whoever you are, get out. I'm calling my security." He swiped and tapped a couple more times.

"I'm someone who wants to find Miraluna Rose. If you care about her, you'll help me." I didn't know if that was true. Maybe the best thing for her would be to stay lost. But it was the best thing for me to say. "You've got my contact."

The door sensors swung it open as I approached, and I stepped out into the hellish heat of midday.

CHAPTER 4

The next spot on my list was Las Aromas, an upscale medical spa near Pacific Palisades, the kind where the rich and famous go for semi-legal boosts to their bodies and their egos. I decided to walk in as a customer. Las Aromas was housed in one of those glass and steel monstrosities off Vicente that were stylish back in the days when we got real rain. A discreet sign in embossed metal read, "Infusions. Injectables. Implants. Sculpturing." The kind of things that could turn your face into a taut, shiny mask if it wasn't done right. A lot of money had been spent on the waiting room to assure the customers that it would be done right.

Despite all the glass windows, the reception room was chilly as a meat locker, if the meat locker had been decorated by a posse of eight-year-old girls with an unlimited budget. The walls were paneled in rose-tinted glass that glowed softly. Sunset cloudscapes floated among screens mounted on the walls on either side of the room. Someone had decided that chaise lounges as fat as caterpillars and covered in fabric woven to have the texture of rose petals set the right tone. The floor was covered with what looked like skin. Baby skin. It gave gently under my shoes as I walked up to the receptionist's desk.

The desk was fronted by a solid slab of marble with rosy veins and topped with a three-inch-thick sheet of polished glass. A wall-to-ceiling aquarium covered the wall behind the desk, backed with a sheet of jagged rose quartz. The amount of water in the aquarium alone was pretentious. The school of jellyfish floating in the artificial current made it offensive. There hadn't been jellyfish in the wild for decades.

The whole setup made me feel like I'd walked into a whale's womb—and it had distracted me from the woman behind the counter. When she murmured, "Welcome to Las Aromas," I finally took her in.

She was quite an advertisement for the place. Implants, sculpturing, injections, and infusions—it looked like she'd had them all. And often. Her forehead was high, and her hairline started way back beyond where the forehead curved up and away from her face. A row of small, ball-shaped implants ringed the crest of her forehead, each of them painted with fluorescent green paint that stood out even in the relentless pink light. More implants like the spines on an iguana's back ran along the top of her arms, dwindling in size as they spread out over the back of her hand. She was wearing something thin and white that teetered between medical uniform and couture; her breasts bulged obscenely against the fabric. She'd probably been good-looking before fashion took over.

The look she gave me was flat and unwelcoming. "Yes?"

"I need a massage."

"Do you have an appointment?"

I leaned my arm on the pristine quartz of her reception counter. I knew it would leave a damp mark. "No. I was just passing by and realized how tight my shoulders are." I knew she knew this was bullshit. No one just passes by anywhere any more.

She summoned up a tight, satisfied smile. "I'm sorry, no appointments are available."

I leaned a little closer to her, playing my gaze along the ridge of implants along her skull. She was wearing special contacts, too, I noticed, that made her irises look like slits. "Maybe I'll wait. You might have a cancellation."

"Very unlikely."

"I'll wait anyway."

She looked a little panicked. "You can't."

"Sure I can." I looked around at all the rosy opulence. "I'll wait in your lovely waiting room."

I parked myself in one of the caterpillar lounge chairs and got out my mobile. She sat back down and stared at the big screen at her desk. I discretely snorted some oxytocin. I thought of the Parrot. He didn't need any fancy modifications. He was complete and beautiful.

An hour went by. No one came in or went out through the single door to the left of the receptionist's desk.

I hoisted myself out of the folds of the caterpillar and walked back to the desk. The green-studded receptionist popped up when she heard me coming, swiping her screen to blank it.

"I have to say, your place does not look busy. Are you sure you can't squeeze me in?"

Her face did something interesting as it tried to frown around the studs in her forehead. I just watched. Finally, she gave up on trying to compose a forbidding-enough expression. "I'll check," she said through her teeth.

She slipped through the door into the back, opening it just enough for her to fit through. It was a good ten minutes before she came back. Splotches of red on her cheeks ruined her scaly style. "We do have an opening. Massage with Deirdre."

"Thank you so much," I said politely. No need to twist the knife.

"It's twenty-five coins."

I shrugged and touched my mobile to the screen embedded in the desk. I wasn't used to celebrity pricing, but Thin Man certainly was. Iguana Girl pointed to the door next to her desk. "Deirdre will meet you inside."

The door opened on a long corridor with a very high ceiling. Waiting inside was another girl who'd gotten too enthusiastic with her modifications. I'd seen pictures of people who'd done extreme things to their bodies for fashion, but I'd never been this close to one of them, let alone two.

I let my eyes travel down from her head to her shoulders, figuring she'd spent all this money to make people stare. I took in the bald head delicately tattooed with a pattern of opalescent spots. She'd shaved her eyebrows, too, and ringed her already-large eyes with black to make them seem enormous. Plastic surgery had trimmed her nose to a nub, and injections had ballooned her lips. She looked like something that should be clinging to a damp tree. I wasn't at all sure I wanted her hands on me.

She waited patiently until I was done staring. "Do you like it?" she asked then.

I shrugged. "You're very unusual."

Her pillowy lips curved up. "Follow me."

We went down the hallway, my shoulders brushed by the sheets of silky white fabric that festooned the ceiling and dripped down the walls to meet the floor, which was covered in moss-green tile. A breeze from nowhere rustled the drapery, bringing along a scent of spice and flowers. Las Aromas, I supposed. Aside from the faint sound of the moving air, the building was dead silent. Deirdre moved like a woman, at least, I noticed as I watched her hips.

We passed two doors on the right before she stopped at a third. She opened it and stood aside to let me go in first. The room I entered was more like an opulent bedroom than a place for therapy. It was a good eighteen feet deep and twelve wide, with the same white walls, high ceiling and mossy floor as the hallway. The far wall was paneled with screens showing sunset on a beach, a beach from a time when beaches were alive. The ocean was blue; palm trees swayed in a breeze; pelicans dove.

In front of it was a platform bed big enough for three people. It was covered simply in a white cotton blanket and edged with fluffy pillows. To my right, water from a wall-mounted fountain trickled into a spa pool containing more fresh water than I'd ever seen—except for the aquarium in the lobby.

The left side of the room looked more like a treatment area. It was lined with built-in cabinetry faced in chrome. A glass counter held a chrome sink and a line of glass and chrome canisters. And there was a treatment table, a fancy one with chrome legs and an excess of knobs, dials, and levers all tucked neatly against the frame.

Deirdre took a white robe from a row of hooks next to the door and handed it to me. "Do you want me to leave while you undress?"

I was curious, not knowing the routine in spendy spas. "I don't care." She stood, still and relaxed, and watched me impassively as I unzipped my shirt and shrugged it off. When I looked around for a place to put it, she held out her hand. I slipped off my shoes, and she bent to take those, too, moving them onto a shelf against the wall under the hooks. I unzipped my pants and stepped out of them and my shorts at the same time. I didn't have to worry about being erect. That's over for me.

"Please lie down," she said, extending her hand toward the table. "It's a massage, yes?" I nodded. "What are your treatment goals?"

"I guess, muscle tension."

She nodded, moving to the table and pressing her hand against my shoulder to get me to lie down. So far, the spa seemed like the real deal. Except for the weirdness of the staff and the lack of patrons. Delicate fingertips pattered against my brow, causing me to close my eyes despite my need to stay alert.

"You don't seem very busy here," I said.

"We have an elite clientele," she murmured. Her fingers pitter-pattered their way over my eyelids and down my cheeks, meeting under my chin. Her fingertips were broad, and they seemed to cling to my skin, pulling it away from the muscle in a way that made it tingle nicely. She joined her hands underneath the base of my neck and put pressure against my skull. I heard my bones creak. This woman did seem to know her massage.

"Your spa was recommended by a friend of mine."

"Really?"

"Her name is Miraluna Rose. Do you know her?"

There was no change in the pressure or rhythm of her hands on my shoulders. "I couldn't say."

"You don't know if you know her?"

"Client privilege. I really can't say."

"The owners run a tight operation, don't they?"

She didn't reply, just kneaded her fingers more deeply into the back of my neck, letting the weight of my head push against them.

"Who owns this place, anyway?"

"It's a corporation," she murmured. "That's all I know." She moved to an LED-studded, white metal box resting on the counter and pushed some buttons. Mist began to flow out of tiny openings along the ceiling, bringing down that same flower scent. She ran her hands over my face, closing my eyes again. "Be still. Relax."

"Just one thing," I said, trying to catch her enormous hazel eyes. "The woman I'm asking about—Miraluna Rose—she's in trouble. I'm trying to help her."

She looked back at me with the same goggle-eyed expression she'd worn throughout our encounter. "Relax," she said again, this time in a whisper.

Funny enough, I did. I woke up an hour later, feeling strange. My muscles seemed to hang off my bones, and I struggled to focus my mind. I took a couple of deep, perfumed breaths and looked at Deirdre. This time, she met my eyes. "Miraluna Rose," I said. "I'm trying to help her."

She looked away. I clenched my hands. I'd learned nothing.

By the time I'd walked out the door, whatever she'd done to me had worn off. I was getting twitchy. I needed to see the Parrot.

But there was one more thing I needed to do. The best way to find something is to build a matrix—connect the dots. I'd accumulated some data points, now I needed to see how they fit together.

The sun outside Las Aromas was blistering. Brown scurf hung down over the steel-gray ocean, turning its tepid tides dingy. The wide boulevard was deserted except for a few Googles, their bodies dulled by the astringent air. I stepped into the street and motioned to one of the Googles. It took me to Los Feliz, where I caught the high-speed rail to San Francisco.

CHAPTER 5

The Everything Archive was housed in what used to be the Officers' Club in the San Francisco Presidio. The complex of nineteenth century buildings was nestled in sand dunes on bluffs overlooking the Golden Gate. I'd heard it was a park once, before the Big Change. There'd been a bridge there, too, but it had been bombed, and with all the passenger drones working the skies, it hadn't seemed worth rebuilding it.

The Everything Archive was purported to hold the entirety of the world's digital information. I believed it. You could access the Archive from anywhere, of course, but there were two reasons it was worth making the trip to the physical location.

First, was the bandwidth. The actual information was all archived on cloud servers with backups on several satellites in different orbits, so that if a comet or a well-aimed rocket took one out, there was plenty of redundancy. But the Archive building held arrays of super-servers that had priority relationships with the cloud servers. You could retrieve information in nanoseconds instead of the second or two it would take from my personal system.

The second reason—the big reason—was the Librarian. He was a sentient robot housed in a humanoid, silicone gel form. He had a head, neck and chest mounted on a real-mahogany stand so that his head was at approximately eye level for the average human. The Librarian had been carefully modeled to look the way Argus Kavinoky, the Archive's founder, had looked in his prime: shaggy sandy hair just starting to go gray; a high, balding forehead that made him look wise; brown eyes with laugh lines at their corners that made him look kind. He wore wire-rimmed glasses, like Kavinoky had, just for looks. His computer vision was no doubt perfect.

He didn't only look like the original archivist; to a great extent, he *was* him. When Kavinoky got his fatal cancer diagnosis, he'd begun offboarding his personality. He'd hired a team of AI researchers who developed complex ladders of questions designed to capture not only what he knew and what he thought about stuff, but also how his mind made connections among bits of knowledge.

Kavinoky died twenty years ago, but the development team was still fiddling with the AI's deep-learning algorithms. They swore the robot was not only self-aware but also pretty much like Kavinoky. But I'd heard his widow wanted nothing to do with the ersatz version. It was both too much and not enough like the real thing.

I'd never known Kavinoky, but I liked the Librarian just fine.

The joke about the Librarian was that he was just a figurehead. Besides him not having a body, you didn't need him to look up things, although he might be helpful for some of the less-sophisticated tourists who might find their way in here. But he was fun to talk to. He had a sunny personality that seemed real but no trace of the agony I'd expect a real person to feel about being powerless to move through the world.

He smiled when he saw me come through the door. "Finder, wut up?" Although they keep his knowledge base updated, the Librarian's personality reflects Kavinoky's, so his linguistic style is out of date.

"Looking to slurp some of that deep learning out of the sky, my friend."

The AI chuckled. "Always looking, right, Finder?"

"That's why it's my name. Checkit, have you seen the North Kardashian sex stream?" The Librarian loves low culture.

"No, how'd I miss that? Let me check it out." The pause while he accessed the cloud was infinitesimal. "I dunno, the lady is kind of old to be getting up with that shit."

"You should talk, old fellow."

The Librarian's eyes crinkled. "Was that a diss?"

"That was a diss indeed, my friend. Listen, I need to access the corporate databases."

"You know I need an authorization code."

"Of course." I swiped my mobile and held the screen up to his left retina.

"Okay," he said, shaking his head. "I don't know how you do it."

"And you don't want to know. See you in a bit."

He buzzed me through the gate, made to look like an old-fashioned wooden gate but capable of withstanding several tons of force. I went into the big, dark room beyond. Lights softly flickered on as I passed by until I sat down at a screen toward the back. I let its reader scan my mobile and then my irises for verification before settling back to untangle the threads of corporate ownership and profit.

But first, I wanted to look at the official identity of BruceWayne, or as I preferred to call him, Thin Man. I followed skeins of social logins and relationships, and then I cracked a highly sensitive government database that was supposedly inviolable. There, I found his true, legal identity. He was Jasper Litwak, an eighty-nine-year-old native of Poland who'd made his first fortune in drone control software. He'd moved to the States forty years ago, and made a couple more fortunes. Nothing surprising there.

But getting Thin Man's official name allowed me to track back down those social graphs. I found a parallel social ID that was just as developed as that of the ultra-wealthy technologist. The name on this identity was Diverdown47, and this version was just as wealthy but a lot darker.

There was participation in the secret parts of Reddit, the parts the company doesn't let its advertisers see. There were videos from Extreme Sexual Combat bouts. Subscriptions to illegal suicide streaming services. The kind of deeply disturbing and interdicted entertainment that only the very rich can access.

I got a whiff of ozone as exhaust fans kicked on, counteracting the carbon dioxide I was emitting with a susurrus of cool air. I was still alone in the Archive; the Librarian was quiet, thinking deeper and more complex thoughts than I could comprehend.

Next, I queried Diverdown47's activities against the corporate databases. Six months ago, he'd invested in a Series B round of funding for a startup called ReMe, kicking in a quarter of a million coins. I'd heard of ReMe, of course. It cloned the rich to create spare parts. It had made a lot of waves when it began production.

Was there a connection between Jasper Litwak, alias Thin Man, alias Diverdown47, and Las Aromas? I found it in Nihelroush. Nihelroush owned the building where the spa was located, and he also had a substantial investment in ReMe.

The Librarian turned his head when he heard me open the gate. "Find what you were looking for, Finder?"

"Yes, I did."

"You always do. Stay cool, man."

"You too, meathead." The Librarian loves it when I call him that, no doubt because he's synthetic.

CHAPTER 6

The Parrot had been busy, and not in a good way. Sometimes, when I leave him, he just dozes the time away; sometimes he gets antsy. Like this time. He'd shredded one of the sofa cushions and then carefully deposited the shreds around the room in a spiral pattern with the widest part of the spiral beginning at his bed and narrowing down to its end at the door. That's the Parrot right there. Dumb and smart at the same time. Dumb, because if he was bored, he could have turned on the big screen and watched a feed; I've shown him how. Smart, because he wanted to give me a message—and I'd gotten it.

"Sorry, bud," I told him. "You would have hated it."

Satisfied with what he'd done and my reaction, he swooped to my shoulder and nuzzled my neck. I reached up and found the place where his wing met his chest, stroked downy skin. Then, I walked to the closet, took out a wand, and connected it to the central vacuum outlet.

The Parrott yapped, lifting himself off my shoulder while keeping his grip. "Ouch! Cut it out. You knew this had to happen." When the vacuum began to hum, the Parrot started flying around, diving erratically. The vacuum drives him crazy. See what I mean? Dumb.

By the time I'd cleaned up all the mess, I'd had it. I was frazzled—from being outside for so long, from the bullet train itself. I don't care what they say; people aren't made to move so fast. I cut up some tofu for me and the Parrot, set the gel bed for a heat/vibration program that would gradually settle me, inhaled some oxytocin, and began to prepare my nighttime meds. Miraluna Rose would have to wait until tomorrow.

* * *

The last thing I wanted to do the next morning was head back to Laxangeles, so I decided it was time to hack into Miraluna Rose's accounts. I set up a cracking program and let it run in the background while I looked more closely at the woman's activities over those two days before she vanished. Maybe there were things I could accomplish over VirChat.

Why don't I do all my business virtually, like most people? It all comes down to the meat. For all the ways we can stay virtually connected anytime, anywhere, something weird happens when two humans get in the same physical space. It's physiologically harder to lie—and harder to deceive me. There's something, maybe an odor or a pheromone or an electrical charge, that I can pick up when I'm in proximity to someone.

That kind of thing tells me more than HD ever could. It's also how I differentiate my business. I do the ugly, unpleasant face-to-face work most people don't want to. You can be sure that Thin Man had exhausted all the digital channels before he showed up at my warehouse.

Once my cracking program had gotten into Miraluna Rose's accounts, I merged them all, with all their data, and then put a deep learning tool to work uncovering correlations and connections. It took the program about seven minutes to chart her eight most important virtual connections. I did a simple sort according to communication channel and then applied one of my finest analytics tools: my intuition.

There was one connection that came in bursts on Twitter: post and responses, never a retweet, a few times a day for a few days, then nothing for a few more days. That said emotion to me, and emotion said friends.

I threaded my way back through the layers until I found a true identity. Clarissa Pellissier, CEO of Adnomyx, a "platform for media optimization." The kind of company that's responsible for beaming ads for VR dating onto my mobile.

I knew about Pellissier; she was a star in tech circles. She'd risen through the engineering ranks at Adnomyx to take over as the CEO at a time when the company was faltering. She'd ruthlessly cut staff and perks, gaining a reputation as a cold calculator. But she'd turned the company around. Its market cap was now bigger than a third of the world's countries.

I messaged her at her office, and got a voice pingback from an automated assistant.

"Hello! This is Serenity! Please say the name of the person you are trying to reach."

"Clarissa Pellissier," I said, enunciating all syllables.

"Okay. Clarissa Pellissier. Is that right?"

"Yes!"

"Let me see if I can find her. Please say your name."

I picked a name from midway down Pellissier's social graph. "Adrian Forte."

"Please hold on…Adrian Forte. I'll see if she's available." So stately and old fashioned, the casual, human-sounding AVR. Nowadays, most systems just use a quick menu.

The chirpy voice came back. "I'm connecting you with…Clarissa Pellissier."

A cool, authoritative voice said, "Hello?" and then her face resolved on my screen. It was fresh and intelligent. Even through the screen, I could see softness behind a hard front.

I had my video on so she could see I wasn't Adrian. In the instant before she could touch the End button, I said, "Wait!" I let the urgency show on my face.

"Who are you?"

"I'm a finder."

"A finder." She made a show of turning that over in her mind. "What are you looking for?"

I gave her back a show of discretion. "Can we meet in person?"

She laughed. "Are you out of your mind? Who does that?"

"I do that."

She stared at me. "Why?"

"It makes my job easier. People are still wired to be with other people."

"It's out of the question."

I leaned in. "I told you I find things. Sometimes it's things people want; sometimes it's things I can use as currency. I found some things about you."

She scoffed. "I don't think so. I run a multi-million-coin company. You wouldn't believe the attacks the bad guys put against everything I do. Are you claiming you hacked us?"

"No—although it would be easy enough."

"*Phuff!*"

I ignored that. "I followed some information trails, connected some dots of data. And found, for example, that Adnomyx has been aggregating data about people's behavior into a massive database that lets you predict mass-market activity."

She shrugged, but red flushed her chest above the scoop neck of her ivory-colored top. "It's all anonymized. The data is certainly a competitive advantage, but it's not illegal to store it."

"It is illegal to use it to manipulate the bitcoin markets."

Her jaw dropped for a second before she got control of herself. I watched her breathe, trying to slow her heart rate. I waited.

Finally, she said, "The executive who did that was terminated, and her social ID was wiped of any cred related to our company."

"Your company grabbed the data, and it's still holding onto it. That's enough for an indictment under privacy laws."

She held her ground, but I saw the defeat. "What do you want?"

"I just want to talk to you in person. I need your help."

She sighed. "All right." She looked down for a moment at a screen somewhere. "Can you be at my office in an hour and a half? I have thirty minutes then."

"I'll be there."

Her eyes went to the Parrot, nosing around on a shelf behind me. "What's that?"

"That's the Parrot."

"Bring him."

CHAPTER 7

I read up on Pellissier. She'd gotten a lot of press for being the first CEO to live at her company headquarters. She'd made a big deal about how it was a "seamless integration, a nexus of passion points," yada yada. Some people thought she wanted to prove that a woman could be as always-on as the young studs. The upshot was a corporate campus that spread leisurely from a Hyper Glass-walled office section fronting the parking lot back into a low-slung travertine-and-glass apartment nestled among a few coddled oak trees. I checked out the photos on design sites. It didn't scream money, but it made its point.

The office building was more impressive in real life. Its proportions were tricky. From a distance, it looked massive. As I stood on the paved entryway, it seemed to shrink into comfortable human scale. The tang of burnt eucalyptus stung my nostrils.

I waved my mobile at the screen on a massive glass door rimmed in chrome, and it swung open into a wide lobby guarded by a long desk made of real wood. Screens lined the back wall where it met the eighteen-foot ceiling, displaying rapidly changing montages of city streets. More wood had been opulently scattered around in the form of straight chairs cushioned in lush white plastic.

The woman behind the desk had the moist skin of the young and well-paid. She gave me a serene smile that let me know just how happy she was to be employed by Adnomyx. Her smile warmed up a bit when she looked at the Parrot. "Hi, there."

I generally see a positive reaction to the Parrot as a sign of intelligence and confidence.

"I'm here to see Clarissa Pellissier."

A carefully epilated eyebrow went up. Pellissier could hardly get many walk-ins. She swiped a screen, tapped and looked up. "Just a moment and someone will escort you." She held out a tablet. "Would you mind giving us a handprint?"

"Not at all." Some people resent it, but I never do. I'm happy to contribute to the Fund of All Data. I use it enough.

Another moist and well-groomed young person appeared through a set of doors and stopped when he saw me with the Parrot on my shoulder. "Um," he said.

"It's all right, Taye," said the receptionist. "He's here to see Ms. Pellissier."

He looked impressed, although he avoided looking again at the Parrot. Chimeras seem to spark an atavistic fear in some people. "Come with me, please."

He led me down a curving corridor carpeted in teal. The wall on our left was purple and punctuated with glass doors; I could see rows of workstations behind them. On our right, patterns etched into the Hyper Glass pixelated the view of the other office complexes nearby. We walked for a few minutes, occasionally passing through sets of double doors that automatically unlocked with a click when my guide approached them. The last corridor ended at a simple wooden door, an elegant slap of fine-grained dark wood polished to a satin sheen. My escort picked up a rounded tube of polished stone that was lying in a copper bowl on a shelf mounted next to the door and tapped on the door twice.

The woman who opened the door didn't really go with the luxe digs and the high-powered gig. And she was a lot softer-looking than she'd appeared in the carefully lit, posed photos in the design spreads. Her hair was what they would have called honey-colored in the old days, carefully shaved on the sides but looser at the crown than was fashionable. Her facial tattooing was muted, just some grey tracery at her temples, a spatter of blue dots on her left cheek and a rose hue outlining delicate lips. She'd dusted her face and hands with pearlescent powder that made her seem like an expensive candy.

"Thanks, Taye," she said to my escort. "We're good." He ducked his head and melted away. She eyed the Parrot but didn't say anything. I felt him lean toward her; he *greeped* in greeting. "Come in."

The foyer of her apartment was as big as my workshop. Muted lighting picked up highlights from a wall of objects displayed on floor-to-ceiling shelves of dark wood. I clocked ephemera from a few different centuries. Beyond it, a living room stretched into the distance, lit by the carefully polarized sunlight coming from a window wall. It was a formal-looking room, laid out for sedate cocktail parties with several groupings of seating and no sign of screens. Toward the back, away from the wall of windows, was an immense, cushy couch lined with plush pillows upholstered in oriental fabrics. No wipeable plastic here. Two people were lolling on it, ignoring my entrance. So I ignored them, to be polite.

Pellissier led me to a pair of upholstered armchairs that had the rickety look of genuine mid-century modern. They faced each other across a small but solid table of the same ilk, and lights in the ceiling made the grouping into a little island in the big room.

She swiped her watch, and a girl appeared carrying a tray with two glasses of water. The servant was slight and dark, dressed in the casual clothes a 5-percenter would wear to the mall. Moisture beaded on the outside of the glasses. There was an icy-looking carafe on the tray, as well. I took a glass and let the chill travel through my hand.

I'd been carefully ignoring the other people in the room—maybe security or some other henchpeople, I supposed. Now, I snuck a look, and the chill traveled up my spine and grabbed the back of my neck.

Distorted faces watched me with vacant eyes. They were eerily like Pellissier's face with something vital missing. The bodies, dressed in identical loose shifts, sprawled in ungainly postures.

I looked away. "What are you doing with clones?"

She looked uncomfortable. "We call them the Cousins."

"Call them what you want. They're still clones."

Cloning is tightly regulated, and the clones themselves are supposed to be locked up in licensed facilities. When ReMe was ready to produce commercially viable clones—the company called them Absolutes—there was a lot of panic. The regulators hadn't really thought it through, and the media erupted with worst-case scenarios. Would clones kill their primaries and take over their identities? Would people fall in love with their own clones and marry them? Could a clone be elected president?

The only way ReMe could get the FDA to let it start clone production was by making sure none of these nightmares could ever come to pass. So, it developed a way to edit their DNA, stripping out parts while still leaving a viable organism. The most important thing ReMe's Absolutes were missing was the prefrontal cortex—the thinking brain. Clones can feel pain and pleasure, they can desire things, but they can't tell themselves stories about why they feel that way. They can't plan, and they can't make predictions about the future. The scientists say this means they're not conscious. I'm not so sure.

The other thing ReMe did was a lot simpler. Even a clone without a prefrontal cortex might be able to kill or pass for human. So the company took away one of humanity's greatest advantages: fingers—and it took away toes for good measure. A clone's hand ends where a human's fingers begin. Its palm can hold things well enough, but it doesn't have the precision necessary to manipulate its environment. And, with no fingers, it can't swipe or tap screens. A clone's foot has five little nubs for toes, enough to let it shamble around on its own but not enough to give it the balance to run or to look human when it's on the move.

There was an attack-of-the-clones meme that spread for a while in the media after they were introduced, but that's died down. Because they're only licensed for medical procedures like transplants, most of us have only seen clones in feeds. This was the first time I'd seen one in the flesh.

They were grisly. As far as I could tell, neither of them looked much like Pellissier. They had the same pale, silky hair, but their faces were broad and puffy, and their bodies seemed loose and blowsy compared to her tight little body. They sprawled against each other on the divan, flailing their spatulate limbs aimlessly.

"I have legitimate medical need," she said.

"Really?"

"Really."

I must have looked more outraged than I meant to—and for some reason, that didn't make her more defensive, like it might have. The meat thing. She swiped her watch, and I heard a tiny voice say, "What, Mommy?"

"Can you come in here, baby?"

"Okay, Mommy."

She watched me defiantly until a small boy entered the room. I felt the Parrot shift; something about the boy didn't smell right to him.

He was scrawny and weak. His arms, bare below the short sleeves of a knitted shirt, were mottled with bruises. She held out her arms and he pressed himself gently against her, as though he had a small bird in his chest pocket that he didn't want to crush. I could see how her own arms, slim and ropy with muscle, encircled him with the barest touch. She looked at me over his head. "Cornell, say hello to our visitor."

The boy turned to look at me. His eyes were bruised deep into their sockets. He didn't seem taken aback at seeing a stranger in the flesh. "Hello," he said. "I have leukemia. Everyone wonders, so I just say it right away."

"It's nice to meet you," I said.

Then, he saw the Parrot. He eyed him with wonder. I could feel the Parrot leaning out, getting closer to the boy, making little chuffing noises as he huffed the Cornell scent.

"That's a pretty bird," the boy said, turning his own beaky face up. "Does it talk?"

"Not in words."

"Does it bite? I have to be careful."

The Parrot is very particular about how he's touched, and he'd never seen a child before. I've only met a couple myself; they're too expensive and delicate for the average person. I felt curiosity but no fear from the Parrot and decided it would be a good learning experience for all of us. "Go ahead and touch him. Just be careful. Use your finger on his chest."

I held my arm up to the Parrot so he could climb on, and then lowered him near the boy. Cornell raised a phthisic finger and gently moved aside the green fur to stroke the skin. I felt the Parrot's grip on my arm rhythmically loosen and then grip again, a sign of pleasure.

But then the Parrot made a move as though he was going to climb onto Cornell's shoulder, and the boy reared back. The Parrot *squirked* and then settled on my arm.

"I have to be careful," Cornell said again.

Pellissier gave him a gentle push. "Why don't you go cuddle?"

The boy moved on his stick legs to the divan and climbed on, nudging the two clones to make room between them. They flopped their arms and made ineffectual pushing motions with their slabbed feet, settling back into place with him nestled between them. Cornell pushed his face against a tit, his hands stroking their skin, their own pitiful hands patting him as they chuckled and gurgled over him.

I felt sick.

"The Cousins are close enough to be his marrow donors," she said. "But it isn't helping."

"It's illegal to keep them around."

"My lawyers have a different opinion. You think the Tissue Bureau doesn't know? They can't afford to take it to trial." The hard front was hardening up again.

"You people. You think money lets you do whatever you want."

"Kind of."

"Even so. Why keep them here, where the child has to look at them?"

She looked sad. "Have you ever seen a clone storage facility?"

"No."

"Few people have. No one wants to think about it too much." She leaned toward me, a flush starting on her chest and spreading up her neck. "They're horrible places. I wanted to give the Cousins a real home. It's the least I can do for them when they're giving so much to us." She looked over at the ghastly huddle on the divan. "Besides, Cornell doesn't see them the way you do. Look. He loves them. That's the way it should be."

I shrugged, not sure where my distaste was coming from; but showing it wouldn't make her more willing to help me. "So. Why I came."

"Yes." I could see anger welling up behind the cool mask. "Blackmail."

"I need your help, that's all. Miraluna Rose has disappeared, and I'm trying to find her."

"I don't know who that is. Is that her primary social name?"

"I think you know her. Your social graphs have a 47 percent congruence."

She looked bemused instead of outraged. "How did you get access to my social graph?"

"It's my job. I also accessed her accounts. You've communicated with her recently on several channels."

She looked irked. "That's outrageous. I can have you arrested."

"And I can get Adnomyx investigated. Unauthorized use of personal data on a scale like yours would tank this company."

Her face was flushed red under the opalescence. She glanced over at Cornell, snuggled in with her clones. I saw her make the calculation. "Who's paying you to find her?"

"I can't tell you that."

"Well, I can't tell you where she is. I don't know."

"Give me something. A place to look. Someone to talk to."

"If you want to do some investigating, you should take a look at ReMe."

There was something in her voice, even face-to-face, but I couldn't quite get what it was.

"Why?"

She stood up. "It might inform your work," she said, all CEO again. "And I have my own work to do." She swiped her mobile. "Taye will escort you out."

CHAPTER 8

The Parrot was getting hot. Neither the bird nor the dog in him was good at temperature regulation. So our next stop was a kuhlhaus. There's nothing like climate change to create new business models, and as the Big Change really took hold, so did the kuhlhaus concept. There were times when the heat got so bad that accessing a kuhlhaus could mean the difference between life and death, especially for people who couldn't afford Hyper Glass windows.

The attendant, a pale man with etiolated limbs and a bleached tuft of snow-white hair, looked like he never left the premises. He stared avidly at the Parrot. "Can I touch it?" he asked wistfully.

I felt sorry for him. A lot of people have never even seen a live animal, and we're hard-wired to crave being around them. But still. "Sorry, it's a licensed comfort bioid." The Parrot *greeped* at him, and that seemed to cheer him up.

The 70-degree room was almost empty—most patrons of these things are looking for a more serious chill. I set the Parrot down underneath a low, translucent plastic table, where he wouldn't be conspicuous, and sat back on a matching chaise. This was an upscale kuhlhaus, with a frosty blue décor designed to heighten the effect of the cool air. Some of the lower-end ones are just rooms with benches where tired old folks can ward off heatstroke for as long as their coins hold out.

The Parrot splayed out on the floor, bringing his belly into maximum contact with the chilled surface. I watched as his panting slowed, felt my heartbeat slow as well.

The only other patron was a woman whose smooth brow and taut cheeks were belied by the sagging folds of wrinkled skin on the naked arms folded outside the fluffy blue-white towel she had wrapped herself in. "Nice dog," she said.

"Mmph," I replied forbiddingly. I took out my mobile and swiped through my messages. A molecular biology researcher at the Karolinska Institute wanted to hire me. I sent an automated response saying I was engaged. Thin Man wanted a status update. I replied with a bill for forty-five coins. There was an alert on a new patent application for an artificial genetic sequence, another one for a variant of *Pseudomonas*. I read the application through while me and the Parrot cooled off. Then, I prepared to follow Miraluna Rose to the next stop on her journey before she disappeared.

Streetly showed the West Hollywood address as a shabby bungalow hunkered down in a row of identical little houses. It was registered to the New Church of the Expansive Essence. A quick search told me the church was founded by someone named Roh Maxman. It was duly registered as a religious organization, which meant I'd have to do a little extra work to dig into its membership and finances. I was feeling too relaxed from the cool air to bother. I could do it on the way home if it seemed worth it.

The front desk sent a subtle *bong* sound to my device to let me know our time was up, and we headed back out to face the broiling day.

* * *

The address was just a Google from the kuhlhaus, in one of those nondescript blocks of houses near Melrose, where the houses had whiplashed from middle-class to million-dollar and then back down. Now it was a neighborhood of old people and poor people who didn't have the means to escape to anyplace away from the permanent meteorological inversion.

We pulled up silently in front. I fed the Parrot a couple of protein snacks and looked around.

At some point, probably as the Big Change was really heating up, someone had shadowed all the windows with deep metal awnings and built out a wide porch from the main entrance. The outsized shades gave the low building the look of a beetle fatally caught out in the bright of day. A huge palm tree, its base as thick as a boulder, its fronds toasted by the heat, squatted in front.

I walked up a path of concrete set between two patches of dusty gravel, the Parrot on my shoulder. He tucked his head under his wing to shield his eyes from the glare. "I know, buddy. It's brutal."

I ducked under the porch's roof into dimness. The old pine door was splintery and gray. Below three tiny windows, a tarnished brass knocker in the shape of a bull's head supported strings of dried herbs. Glazed ceramic pots on each side of the door held dirt that had ossified from decades of baking. We hadn't been able to grow plants outside for many years. It told me that whoever lived here was very old.

I lifted the bull's head and let it fall back against its brass plate. The sharp *plink* of the metal faded as it hit the old, solid wood.

Nothing else changed. The air was motionless and silent. I tasted my own breath and felt the Parrot's against my neck.

I lifted the bull's head and let it fall again. There was no answer. I grasped the big doorknob, shiny around the ball from thousands of palms, turned it and pushed. The door opened. I went in.

The room was dark; chinks of light showed at the edges of heavy curtains and dust motes drifted through them. The smell told me that once this room had been moldy, but the mildew had baked into dust decades ago. It was a decent-sized room, but the actual floor space was small. The walls were lined with a random assortment of shelves and dressers; every horizontal surface was cluttered with objects of all sizes, indecipherable in the gloom. An old-fashioned upholstered couch and two easy chairs crowded into the center. Their upholstery was dotted with patterned cloths that didn't quite hide patches where the stuffing showed through. The Parrot sneezed and ruffled his feathers.

As my eyes adjusted, I made out a form in the chair angled into the farthest corner of the room. It shifted and spoke.

"You enter the hall of the living breath." The voice was an old woman's, so old that it quavered and almost failed on the last word. This breath was barely living. She'd said it without animosity or welcome, simply stating a fact.

I felt like saying, "I come in peace," so I did.

"I feel some peace in you. Not a lot," she replied.

She moved to take up something from the table next to her chair and lit a candle. I winced, thinking of all the carbon dioxide it would put into the air. The room was already stifling. The Parrot rustled and fluttered his wings. I don't think he'd ever seen an open flame. I lifted my hand, moved him off my shoulder and cradled him against my chest.

But now I could see her.

White hair rippled from her scalp to flow over her shoulders and into her lap. I saw strands spilling over the arms of the chair and trailing on the floor. Locks of hair lay like embroidery against a loose white caftan that draped across bony knees and ended just above bare feet that were twisted and knobbed. A silver ring on her big toe had become embedded in flesh.

Her white hair glowing in the candlelight cast her skin into even more shadow. I saw traces of white eyebrow, white lashes ringing pools of blackness.

"Seen enough?" she cackled.

"Not really. I can barely see in here." I sat down in the other armchair. The Parrot nestled into my lap. I could feel his anxiety. I wondered what his superior sense of smell told him about this place.

"You come to the place of the Mountain Queen." Her raspy voice became singsong. "You come to the womb of the mother forest. You seek the world outside of man." She began slowly rocking back and forward in her chair, her bony hands clasped in front of her chest.

I decided I'd better cut her off. "I'm just looking for some information."

"Go look in your machines for answers," she scoffed. "Go away."

"Not every answer is found in a machine."

The black eyes widened. White around the pupils gleamed in the candlelight. "You think you can flatter an old lady?"

"No." Maybe. I was still trying to get a sense of her.

"Do you know how old I am?"

"No," I said patiently.

"Don't you want to know how old I am?"

I sighed. "Sure. How old are you?"

"I'm one hundred twenty-seven."

Now, my eyes widened. Most of the elderly were killed off during the Big Change. The ones who survived were mostly the very rich, who were well-shielded and had the means to ride things out. But even most of them had by now succumbed to time.

She nodded. "You see. You see. I am the fuse in the apple, the bright spark in the womb, the breast of consolation." She was starting to lapse into the chanting thing again.

"I'm trying to find someone you know."

She stopped the rocking and nodding. "Yes, I know. You're the finder."

This was a cheap trick, mirroring back something I'd said in a way that made it seem prescient. It made me impatient with her. "I need you to help me."

"Do you know the New Church of the Expansive Essence?" she asked.

"Yes, I've heard of it. I found it in one of my machines." I couldn't keep the snideness out of my voice. "It's run by Roh Maxman. I assume that's you."

"That's one of the names I'm called by."

"Listen. I'm hot, and it's been a long day. I'm looking for a woman named Miraluna Rose. She's disappeared, and I know that she came to your house on the last day she was seen anywhere. I need to find her, and I need to know what you know about it."

I was frustrated, and the Parrot reacted with a plaintive *klurp*.

"Shush," the woman said, the timbre of her voice suddenly warm and soothing. She reached out her arms. "Give me the bird."

At the same time that I reflexively clasped him tighter, I felt the Parrot wriggling to get free and go to her. I let go, and he hopped from my lap and swooped the short distance into hers.

The Parrot never lets anyone else hold him. He hates strangers as much as I do. But he nestled into her lap, and she bowed her head over him, letting her white hair cover him like a veil. I heard him chortling from the safety of its cocoon. And I felt his pleasure in my own chest, slowing down my breath and warming my skin from the inside out. Only the Parrot can make me feel that way.

Suddenly I was inside the room in a different way. I was seeing her without paying attention to all the accoutrements—the flowing hair, the white robe, the clutter of objects. It was as though I thought I'd been alone and someone else had entered the room without my knowing it.

"There," she said. "Do you feel that? That's better, isn't it?"

"What is it?" I asked. I could feel the Parrot, too.

"It's just connection. It's the essence."

I let myself feel it for a moment. "Miraluna Rose. Should I be looking for her?" I suddenly felt that it was just that simple, just yes or no.

"I don't know," she said, tipping her head back against the chair and stroking the Parrot.

I felt bitterly disappointed. "What do I do now?"

"Wait," she said.

"Will you help me?"

She got up, cradling the Parrot in her arms, and brought him over to me. She held him out, and I took him back, holding my palms against his sides and chest so I could feel the vitality of him.

"Come to my church," she told me. "And bring the bird." She walked over to the door and fished a scrap of paper out of a basket on the shelf there. She held it out to me and opened the door. "You should go now."

* * *

I didn't look at the paper until we were almost home. It was a simple printout, black on white. It said:

Find what you need
New Church of the Expansive Essence
Wednesdays and Fridays, 9 p.m. to midnight
6715 Fountain Avenue

Suddenly, I was enraged—at her and myself. Old people were weird. They'd gone through too much and fallen too far behind. Still, the old lady had pulled some second-rate mind-reading scam on me and somehow I'd gone along with it.

That was the trouble with IRL work; it was too easy to get drawn into someone else's limbic resonance, even for me.

I fumbled in my pockets for my med case and grabbed a couple of modafinils. I emptied one, crushed it, and vaped it. I dropped the second one, and then settled back into the rush. That was better.

The Parrot made a protesting blurt at my fumbling around and then settled back into my lap. He was almost limp, he was so relaxed. His back legs were splayed on either side of my right thigh; his chest rested on the other thigh; and his wings spread loosely. I put my hand flat against his back. The speed was amping up my sense of touch. It was as though I could feel a current coming out of each individual blue hair, running up my arm and hitting up against the countercurrent rushing down my arm from my chest. It made me high.

Inside the high, my mind raced. The old lady knew Miraluna Rose, that was for sure. She could tell me where she was. But she wanted to protect her. Maybe from me. Maybe she *should* be protecting Miraluna Rose from me. If I was going to take her back to Thin Man.

But that was my job. That was what I was being paid for, to find Miraluna Rose and bring her back to Thin Man. That's what a finder does. Suddenly, I didn't like that idea. What had the old lady done to me? Or was this confusion from the drug?

I let my mind spin as I stroked the Parrot. I didn't like Thin Man—I didn't like his sense of entitlement or his dabbling in the dark side of the internet. I didn't know Miraluna Rose, but what I'd seen in her face as she stared into the mirror told me that she was too good for him.

I wasn't going to deliver her back to him. That fact burned through the mind fog. But so did another fact. I was still going to find Miraluna Rose. I wanted to know her.

* * *

The warehouse automation systems automatically kick in the cooling whenever I get within two miles, so it was dark and cool inside. The Parrot had snoozed all the way home, but he perked up when we got inside and *greeped* for his dinner.

Living large on Thin Man's money, I'd ordered a delivery. Grilled shmeat for both of us, with curried algae puffs, seaweed salad, and slices of real avocado. Plus a bottle of Canadian well water. The delivery was waiting inside my chiller lockbox. I divided it up and put the Parrot's meal on his tray. He grabbed the shmeat steak and started ripping it apart with his beak.

"Good, huh?" He didn't answer, too engrossed in the food.

While I ate, I checked my comms. Three messages from Thin Man. I sighed and pinged him.

He came on with video immediately, although he was turned away and talking to someone off-screen. I could see a bank of tables and windows behind him. Some kind of work space. He turned and focused on his screen. He looked pissed. "It's about time," he snapped. "Where have you been?"

"Working."

"Why don't you answer your calls?"

I took a breath, summoning patience. "I am very good at what I do. As you know. That's why you hired me. When I'm working, I need my full attention on what I'm doing."

His eyes popped. "What you're doing is a job for me. *I* need your attention."

"You have it now. What do you want?"

"What I *want* is to know what you've found out. Where is she?"

I picked up the last algae puff and popped it in my mouth. Chewed. Slowly. Sending him a message. "Have you ever heard of the New Church of the Expansive Essence?"

I could practically see fumes rising from the top of his head. "One of those sleazy organizations that prey on the ignorant. We should shut them all down. But what's that got to do with Miraluna Rose?"

"She doesn't attend the church?"

"Of course not," he exploded.

"She's free to come and go though, right?"

"What are you suggesting? Yes, she can go where she wants. But she would never be involved with a whacked org like that."

Pure wishful thinking on his part. Miraluna Rose had a life he knew nothing about, clearly.

"All right."

"All right what? When are you going to bring her back?"

"I've traced everyplace she went on the last day she was seen. Now, I'm following up on them, one by one."

"How long is that going to take?"

People like that. Used to getting what they want. I despised them, but they were my best clients. "It will take until I find her."

"I'll give you three more days."

"Or what?" The modafinil was getting the better of my patience. I was going to find Miraluna Rose whether he was paying me or not. But I didn't want him to know that.

"Or…"

"I'll find her," I told him. "I need four more coins."

He turned red and broke the connection. But when I checked before I went to sleep, the coins had transferred to my account.

That night, the Parrot slept against my chest.

CHAPTER 9

Me and the Parrot arrived at the New Church of the Expansive Essence just as a brown-tinged dusk was falling. I wasn't enthusiastic about bringing the Parrot; his immune system is mostly dog and very strong, but his avian DNA can mess him up when he's exposed to something dodgy. On the other hand, the old lady had specifically told me to bring him. Maybe he was my best way into what she knew.

The Fountain Avenue address turned out to be housed in an actual church instead of the decrepit storefront I'd expected. It was a rundown Christian church, as evidenced by stained-glass crosses in the lower windows. It was a two-story brick building with stone inserts framing the windows and the heavy metal double doors.

I pulled on the right-hand door pull, and the door opened with a creak. I entered a lobby with a granite floor and plain, yellowish walls with another set of double doors, low-grade plastic ones, a sometime-in-the-past cheap replacement for the old lumber that probably had been sold off to pay the bills. Two battered screens flanked the interior doors, showing a montage of promos for workshops and meetings about things I'd never heard of. The lobby was empty, but I heard movement and talking from the other side of the doors.

We entered an open space, as wide as the building and two stories tall. The big room was dim. Tall windows ran along the sides, some of them fitted with Hyper Glass, some with old-fashioned translucent plastic and a couple of them with remnants of the original stained glass, heavily patched with polymer. When the sun shone in, it must be brutal. The air still held the hot stink of hydrocarbons. The Parrot sneezed and ruffled on my shoulder.

Some forty people were milling around at the edges of the room; others were sitting on cheap plastic chairs placed in an uneven ring in the center. I looked for Roh Maxman's blanket of hair but didn't see it. A woman who had been talking with a small group toward the back had looked up when she heard us enter the room and made her way over to us.

"Welcome to the New Church," she said, holding out her hands as though she was going to touch me. I flinched back and the Parrot moved to readjust his grip on my shoulder.

"Oh," she said, looking concerned. "Welcome." She stared at the Parrot. "Thank you."

I looked her over while she was grokking the Parrot. She was clearly a eugie, more politely known as a gene-edited-in-vitro embryo or GEIV. The New Eugenics had been a big thing for a while among the 1-percenters. She had the tall, strong frame, still covered with lean muscle, although she was elderly, as all eugies were. Strong white teeth, blue eyes, platinum hair clipped short, and clear, pale skin marked by Freitak's sarcoma, that cancer that had sneaked in with the positive eugenics. They'd stopped the eugenic programs when that showed up.

She drew her eyes away from the Parrot and met mine. "This is your first time, isn't it? Don't worry. We'll let you come at your own pace."

I wasn't worried about that. I had no intention of coming anywhere near any of them. I just wanted to soften up the old lady and see what Miraluna Rose had been into.

"Whatever," I said.

She stared into my eyes, trying to draw me into some interaction. "My name is Radiance. What's yours?"

"Findhorn," I muttered. I hate saying my name but I didn't want to give away my profession.

Radiance wasn't even carrying a mobile. She was wearing a loose top and matching pants, not as outré as the old lady had been wearing but more flowing than was the fashion. "And your…bird?"

"He doesn't have a name." I could tell the Parrot was relaxed and attentive, but she was starting to bug me. "Where's Roh Maxman?"

"She's doing one-on-ones right now. She'll be out to start our gathering in a few minutes."

Radiance was staring at the Parrot again. I saw one of her hands move up tentatively. I knew she wanted to touch him. I reached up and put one hand protectively on his chest.

"How do I get one of these one-on-ones with her?" I asked.

"Usually she arranges them herself."

"I think she wants to talk to me."

"The best thing would be to go up to her afterward. If she's not too tired, she might see you."

"What's happening now?"

Radiance smiled. "We're all starting to connect. Roh will open the puja in a few minutes."

"Puja?"

"Puja is a worship ceremony. We worship the fire of love in all of us."

"I'll just walk around a little until then," I told her.

"Of course. You're at home here," she said, taking a step back and then turning away.

I walked a slow circuit around the room, keeping my distance from the little groups chatting along the walls as well as those already sitting in the chairs. Besides the chairs, there wasn't much else in the room, just a couple rows of stacked, flat cushions in the far corner, and a few small end tables.

The Parrot fluttered his wings in the close atmosphere, making little *suffles* when his nose caught an interesting scent.

Most of the people were older, somewhere between Roh Maxman and Radiance. I was surprised to see maybe a dozen eugies.

That designer gene fad had been brief and limited to the super-rich. They would be between seventy-five and ninety years old, although they didn't look it. Most eugies lived private lives, meeting face-to-face even less than normal people. Of course, the Freitak's can be disfiguring, that's a big reason. I'd met a couple of them here and there but never seen them in a group.

There was a mix of other people, as well—most of them conventional, a few mods and a smattering of younger gearheads. Some of them were dressed in the street clothes of the affluent, but the majority of them wore some variation of the overly loose and flowing garments Radiance had on. Many people smiled at me or tried to catch my eye as I wandered past them—and many smiled approvingly at the Parrot. I could feel him preening a bit at all the attention. Me and the Parrot don't go into public spaces very much.

A man, dressed in what looked like an antique, white silk sherwani stepped out from a door in the back wall, clutching a brass bowl against the embroidery on his chest. He raised it head-high and hit it with a little mallet. A clear chime rang out, its aftertones shimmering in the heated air. Immediately, everyone in the room headed for the circle of chairs. I followed them, choosing a seat on the arc closest to the entrance.

The man stepped into the center of the circle and rang the chime again. Roh Maxman stepped through the door and made her way into the center of the circle, bowing her head to the man, who stepped back and sat down. The cheesy showmanship made me think even less of the old lady.

She raised her hands shoulder-high, palms facing out, and made a slow, 360-degree twirl, looking at each face in turn. As she faced each person, he or she would lift their hands, palms open as though receiving some kind of magic rays from her gaze.

The sleeves of her robe slid up her arms, revealing the signs of Freitak's. I was startled. Then I did the math. The perfect-embryo fad had begun less than 100 years ago; if Maxman was as old as she said she was, she must be the result of some early experiments in embryo editing.

She lowered her hands, gave a little shiver, and sighed, "Ahhhh."

"Ahhhhh," the group answered.

She took the chair closest to the door she'd entered from, gave a little wriggle and relaxed out of the performative mode she'd maintained since her entrance. "Hello," she said brightly.

"Hello!" everyone answered.

I could feel the Parrot on my shoulder leaning toward the person on my left, a man with cropped silver hair and a thin line of beard. His ear bristled with an old-fashioned media player implant. Even I could smell him a bit, a faint herbal odor inflected with male hormones. I held my forearm up to the Parrot, hoping he'd settle in my lap, but he ignored it. His four feet performed a percussive dance on my shoulder and back. I reached up and pulled him down into my lap. I didn't think this crowd would appreciate it if he started swooping around in the rafters. No, that's not true. I was really afraid he'd fly to someone else.

The old lady raised her hands, took in a deep breath, held it a dramatic moment, looked around mischievously, and then blurted out, "Energized!"

That was the signal for others in the circle to start calling things out.

"Nervous!"

"Grateful."

"Tingling!"

"Turned on!" Everyone chuckled at that one.

"Amazing!"

When the blurting finally died down, the old lady looked directly at me. "Pleasured," she said, trying to draw me into a momentary dyad. I wasn't having it. I gave a curt nod and felt the eyes of everyone else fall away.

Then the Parrot said, "*Greep! Greep!*" And everyone was looking at us again.

One of the most important rules for finding things is to be invisible. Not that me and the Parrot could be invisible here, but if we kept our heads down, people would be more likely to stop paying so much attention to us. I couldn't figure out what was wrong with him. He kept leaning off my lap, like he was dying to check everybody out. I stroked his chest to cool him down.

Maxman gave the Parrot a benevolent smile and began talking. I quickly lost the thread. Something about seven layers, the epigenetics of oxytocin receptors, bodhisattvas, and electromagnetic fields. The typical mishmash of science and new age. I tuned out and looked more carefully at the people around me.

Across from me were a couple of young women who were seriously modded out. They had skull implants emphasized by their shaved heads and heavy use of colorful cosmetics—or maybe they were permanent tattoos. The one with the fuchsia forehead opened her mouth wide with pleasure, and I could see she'd even had her teeth filed to points.

There was a pair of old-fashioned vampire-rocker types, with dyed black hair, faces studded with metal spikes and heavy metal jewelry. And a scattering of people who were simply very old. Pretty much your standard flatlands LA population. Except for all the eugies.

The reedy man in the sherwani carried out a tray with a tall glass pitcher of water and stacks of tiny glasses. I could see condensation on the pitcher, and my mouth watered. He knelt down in front of the old lady and held it out to her.

She grasped the pitcher with both hands and held it up. I could see her skinny arms shaking as she hoisted it.

"When we share, we come closer together," she intoned. "When we share this water, we share ourselves."

A murmur of agreement went around the room. She poured a few drops of water into a glass and handed it to the person on her right, a young woman with mahogany skin who had the asymmetrical haircut and precise eye makeup fashionable among the well-employed. The woman passed it to her right, and it went around the room. By the time it came to me, the glass was warm from all the hands on it. The Parrot sniffed it with interest. I passed it along, resigning myself to a long evening. Finally, with much sighing and murmuring from the group, everyone had received a glass.

"Love," Maxman said. "We are connected." She lifted her glass and drank; so did everyone else.

I didn't want to drink mine. Long ago I'd decided never to drink anything I didn't know the provenance of, and it had kept me healthy through a couple of pandemics. But the Parrot *snurkled* at it. I shrugged and held it up so he could drink. "Your choice, buddy," I told him.

The old lady was looking at us. I wondered if she'd be pissed at me for letting him drink out of her glass, but she smiled.

"Your bird knows more than you do," she said. All her followers chuckled. "Now," she said in a plangent voice, "peace be with you."

Everyone began turning to their neighbors and repeating, "Peace be with you." Some of them were putting their hands on each other, stroking an arm, clasping a hand, even hugging. The people on either side of me both turned toward me at once, and I was caught in a peace sandwich. I gave them each a half-hearted nod, ready to fend off any touching with my forearm. But the Parrot was loving it. He leaned way over in my lap toward the elderly geezer on my right and chortled. The geezer chortled back, and before I could block him, he reached out and stroked the Parrot's head. The bird wriggled out of my grasp and leaped into his lap, nuzzling his head into the guy's armpit.

"Hey!" I said, grabbing him back. Everyone stared. "It's a comfort bioid," I muttered. They all looked sympathetic, which made me seethe.

The old lady stood up and commanded gaily, "Everybody up! Walk, greet, and connect."

Everyone stood up and began to mill around. Immediately, a man wearing a vintage button-down cotton shirt tucked into a kilt moved in front of me and looked me in the eye, a close-lipped smile on his face. The Parrot walked his hind legs down my back, getting a little more space from the man.

"Checkit," I said, looking back at him.

He held his finger to his lips, his eyes locked on mine. "Don't talk. Just look," he whispered.

The irises of his eyes were deep brown, almost blending with the black of his pupils. His eyelashes were lush. I let my gaze travel down his nose, noticing the wiry black hairs peeking out of his nostrils. The man tapped my upper arm with a finger. The Parrot made a clucking noise. When I met his eyes again, he moved his hand back and forth between his eyes and mine. "Watch," he whispered. "Feel our connection."

I spent a couple more minutes waiting to see maybe a glint of light from one of those mahogany orbs. Then Maxman's acolyte tapped his bowl again, its chime the signal for everyone to resume slouching around inside the circle of chairs. I moved slowly, avoiding people's eyes, which isn't hard because I'm so tall. But pretty soon, I got pinned down by a short woman with straight black hair and almond eyes who could have passed for thirteen except for two faint lines at the corner of each eye. I met her gaze as expected and settled in, hoping I didn't get a crick in my neck from looking down.

The third round, I ended up face-to-face with a skeletally thin black man with the few, subtle facial piercings affected by lower-level information workers. He looked into my eyes and then looked at the Parrot.

I felt the Parrot shift on my shoulder, hunkering down against my ear. The bird *greeped* softly, and the man grinned. "*Grrrrp!*" he said, and then laughed. The couple next to us broke their eye lock to glance at him. He laughed again, silently, all the time looking at the Parrot. When the chime sounded, he looked back at me. "Your bird vibes real good," he said.

Everyone took their seats. Maxman stood up, looked around the room, settling people down. There were more deep, sighing breaths. "Aaahh."

"Was that good?" she asked the group. "Did you feel each other?" Heads nodded, breaths sighed out. "That's because we are *made* to be together. When we connect, we are tuning our nervous systems to each other's, synching into resonance. We are wiring our psyches together, forming a neural supercomputer powerful enough to affect permanent change in our environment."

I tuned out. It was more the mystical neuroscience crap. Instead, I thought about Miraluna Rose, confidently striding around her room, and then tried to picture her sitting in this circle, sighing and moaning. I couldn't see it. A squeal from the old lady brought me back.

"Now, everybody! Puppy pile!"

Everyone rushed over to the stacks of pillows and grabbed one or two. They carried them back into the circle, threw them down on the ground and then, unbelievably, got down onto them and began rubbing up against each other, rolling around, flinging their limbs over one another's. My stomach turned.

The grubby hands passing along the water glasses had been bad enough. Now, these people were rubbing skin to skin. I watched hands sliding along cheeks, caressing thighs and arms. Bare soles moved against insteps and traveled under skirts. Lips nuzzled behind ears.

It was crazy dangerous. We'd learned, through millions of pandemic deaths, to keep our distance from each other. Even another's breath can kill. Yet here these people were, behaving as though they were in the twentieth century. It made my skin crawl.

A young woman with wavy red hair extricated herself from the edge of the human worm pile and came over to me. She reached out to take my hand. I shied away. "Connect with us," she whispered. "Come."

I shook my head, feeling the Parrot do that leaning thing toward her. I decided to leave and get at Maxman some other way. Glancing at her, I saw she was murmuring to her acolyte, nodding at me. He moved out of the circle of chairs and came over to speak softly into my ear. "Do you want to wait in back? Roh will see you after she's closed the puja and said goodbye to all the connectors."

I nodded and, keeping a firm grip on the Parrot, followed him to the door at the back of the church.

We entered into a dank little room, windowless gloom lit by a lamp with an old-fashioned incandescent lightbulb. A spindly rectangular table was jammed against the back wall, probably a leftover from the building's churchy days. It held an out-of-date screen, a couple of dusty media trays and a very modern, top-of-the line mobile. A battered wooden dining chair was half-turned to the desk, draped with a wrinkled shawl. Another couple of upholstered chairs were angled into two of the corners, facing into the room. On the wall between them hung a silk fabric with a Krishna figure surrounded by Sanskrit writing and molecular diagrams. The last wall held a sturdy steel shelving unit reaching almost to the ceiling. Behind locked glass doors, an array of blade servers blinked. The shelves below were a jumble of media, little bottles, statues, and dried plant material.

The Parrot took off from my arm and flew to the chair. He made a graceful landing on its back, all four claws grasping its rim. He teetered, and then hopped down to the seat, nestling himself in the shawl. I wondered for a second if the old lady would mind getting some feathers and fur in it. Then I remembered how avidly she'd looked at him. Served her right.

I touched the screen, just for drill, but it was protected. I didn't see the need to crack into it. The only thing I needed to know was why a wealthy, stylish woman like Miraluna Rose had felt the urge to mingle with this lot of misfits. I checked my mobile and clicked on the icon to run a semantic analysis of my hundreds of messages to see if there was anything I needed to look at.

There was a message from The Librarian.

Yo, dude. Spybots were sniffing after you.
Gnarly shit.
Talk to me.

I touched reply.

Checkit.
I appreciate this.
Any idea where they're from?

The Librarian's reply was instantaneous. He's always on and capable of performing an infinite number of simultaneous calculations.

I couldn't penetrate them.
They're seriously defended.
Hard as shit, man.

Did they get into my search history?

Heck, yeah.
They were unstoppable.
I did my best.

No worries.
My ID is heavily shielded.

Watch your back, man.
Just sayin

Thanks, my friend.

Always.

So that was interesting. Either someone had put a digital tail on me or else my digging around in the corporate databases had triggered an alert to someone. Or maybe the nefarious DiverDown47 had hotbots surrounding the identity. It wouldn't be surprising that someone at Nihelroush's or Thin Man's level of wealth had the resources to worm into the databases in order to protect themselves from snooping. Nor was it hard to believe that Thin

Man was following my every move. If I were him, and I could afford it, I'd do the same thing.

The Parrot hopped off the chair and began snuffling around under the table. He's not above eating crap off the floor. "Stop it," I told him. He ignored me, so I ignored him. Sometimes I think he needs to just be a dog.

Outside in the church, the scraping of chairs told me that the ceremony was over. I heard voices outside the door, and then it opened. Roh Maxman was standing there, flanked by the two women with the wild mods—the one with the fuchsia forehead and filed teeth, and her friend, who had a bulging forehead and a face that had been sculpted by surgery to look like a cat. The Parrot *gurked* when he saw them. Maxman smiled at him and then turned to me.

"You wanted to talk to me," the old lady said, making a statement, not a question.

"That's right." I looked pointedly at the two bizarre women flanking her.

"This is Celia," she indicated at the pointy-toothed one, "and this is Carmela."

"Hello," I said politely. I was getting restless. I didn't like the feeling of so much outré female flesh in this close room.

Maxman took a seat in the chair by the desk. I took one of the upholstered chairs, and the other two women piled into the third chair, legs slung around each other. Celia the bird girl put her arm around the other's shoulder.

"What do you want?" Maxman asked.

"I need to find a woman named Miraluna Rose."

"You need to find a woman. Hmmm." The old lady rested an elbow on the desk and leaned her head on her palm. The Parrot jumped up into her lap.

"Hey!" I said.

But she'd already begun stroking him, and he was preening the way he does when he's happy, so I let it be for now.

"Who is Miraluna Rose?"

"You know her," I said. "She's been to your church."

"So many people come here," she said musingly. "Seeking connection."

"She's got green hair. She's beautiful."

"We're all beautiful. Each one of us."

Her woo-woo act was getting to me. "She was here three nights ago. Right before she disappeared. I know you remember her." I leaned forward and grabbed the Parrot off her lap. He *grawked* in protest, but I bundled him back in my lap, stroking him firmly with my palm to let him know he should stay there.

The old lady frowned at me. The two weird girls were watching avidly. She tried to hold my eyes with hers, but I looked away. "I can't feel you," she said.

"I'm not here for your church."

"Why won't you let me feel you?"

"I'm doing a job. If you're not going to help me, I'm wasting my time."

"You're dark. You're dark." She stood up. "Even with the bird. You're dark. Darkness has no place in the temple of love." One of the girls giggled. I glanced at her and while I was distracted, the old lady stood up and plunged something into the base of my neck.

Every muscle in my body clenched, and my vision tunneled into blackness. Some kind of nerve poison. As I blacked out, I thought, "Every good boy does fine." It's the neural pattern that activates my emergency systems. I have artificial neurons spread throughout my brain that can reboot my body chemistry. But it takes a little time to normalize myself.

I woke up in an electronics trash heap in East LA. I still had my mobile. But the Parrot was gone.

The neurochemical reset is a heavy biological trip. It works best when I can stay in a state of rest, letting my systems reach equilibrium in their own time. That wasn't going to happen. I was ambulatory and cognitive, but my amygdala was screaming, *The Parrot, the Parrot, the Parrot, the Parrot.*

I leaned against a bin full of trashed screens and went through my pockets. Nothing was missing. Just the Parrot. *The Parrot.* I gasped in a belly breath to stop the scream from starting again. I emptied a capsule of aniracetam under my tongue. It was the wrong thing to do for my body, but I needed to ignore my body.

My brain flashed with fire. My thinking brain went down. My amygdala, that primitive seat of emotion, grabbed control. I was literally out of my mind, and that was exactly where I needed to be.

The recycling center was protected by an old-fashioned chain-link fence, its double gate padlocked from the outside. I used my pocket laser-saw to cut an opening big enough to walk through. My mobile told me I was east of the river, near the old garment district. I summoned an Uber from downtown and staggered west to meet it.

I thought about the Parrot getting smeared with biologicals in another creepy ritual at the church, but decided it was more likely the old lady would take him home to play with him in private, so that's where I directed the Uber to go.

It wasn't yet dawn, and the bungalows on her street were dark except one down the block, where a big screen reflected its shifting lights onto some isolate's bleary face. The old lady's bunker lowered in the gloom of its overhangs, dark and silent except for the swishing of the fronds of the ancient palm.

I used my mobile to check infrared signatures in the interior. It registered one Maxman-sized body inside, in a room on the north side of the house—and nothing else. The Parrot should have registered if he was in there and alive. My panicking had halved itself by this time. I was still twitchy to get the bird next to me again, but I'd remembered the greedy way the old lady had ogled him and realized she didn't want to hurt him. Still, I'd figured he'd be here, and adrenaline washed my nerves with ice water.

I walked around to the back of the house, not bothering to be quiet. I wanted the old lady to hear me, wanted her to be afraid.

I kicked open the back door and blasted through the kitchen, shoving the table aside and into a short hallway. I put my shoulder to the first bedroom door and it splintered away. A dark form scrabbled out of the bed into a corner on the far side. I grabbed roughly, locking my hand around the woman's upper arm and dragged her into the living room. Still squeezing her arm, I used the other hand to fumble the switch on a lamp and then slammed her onto the floor.

"Where is he?" I shrieked.

It wasn't Maxman. A young girl, skinny legs askew, was sobbing hysterically on the floor. She'd wet the pair of pink, sparkly boy-shorts she was wearing. I had no pity for her.

"Where's the old lady?"

She just blubbered, curling herself into a ball.

"Does she have the Parrot? A bird? Did you see the bird? Where is she?"

The more I yelled, the more she cringed and cried. I was shaking with rage and panic. I grabbed her by the shoulders and hauled her up. I opened the front door and thrust her out into the yard. "Run," I yelled. "Run!"

I stormed through the house, opening closets and yanking cupboard doors. I overturned the water recycling unit and swept the shelves of the cooling unit onto the floor. A gush of self-pity brought me to my knees and I summoned rage to get me up again. I went back into the living room and pushed over a bookcase. Particles of decomposed paper clouded the air. I ripped one of the books apart. I lit the old lady's greasy candle and held loose pages to it until they caught, then set the candle in the pile of books. I waited until the fire burned brightly, then walked down the street and out of the neighborhood. I felt the fire's heat on my back.

* * *

I flagged down a Google, spoofing my ID, and rode north, erasing my GPS record and replacing it with the coordinates of my warehouse. If anyone looked at my mobile, I'd been home all night. The government database would show my true movements, but I doubted anyone would look.

I transferred to a public jet back to Berkeley and then walked the two miles to the warehouse. I was still trembling with all the drugs warring in my body and my mind was a red fog.

The warehouse felt wrong. It had been three years since I'd been in it alone. My need for the Parrot was like a thirst.

I drank an entire liter of the water that was waiting in the recycler. I blended kelp powder, cricket powder, tofu, frozen apple pulp, and water, and drank it down. Then I injected myself with B-12 and T, and took two modafinils. I felt marginally better, physically.

I sat down at my screens.

I'd trashed her den; where would the old lady go? I found nothing else on her in the public data systems—no social profiles, no electronic breadcrumbs. Probably media denial was part of her doctrine. I messaged the Librarian. No one except the Archive staff is supposed to be able to. Although he's recognized as a sentient being, the designers didn't want to give him true autonomy. It had gone to the Supreme Court, where they'd won. But they'd made a back door, just in case. And I had the key. Me and the Librarian have a lot of history.

Dude. Wut up?

I need your help

I had no time and no energy for niceties.

Roh Maxman, head of the New Church of the Expansive Essence. I need to find her fast

Finder you know I can't

Yeah I know but I know you can

Protocols, dude. You have to come in and do it yourself

The Parrot's missing

Oh man that's harsh. What happened?

Maxman grabbed him. I need to find him

I really need to find him

The Librarian was silent for a split second.

739 Citrus Avenue in LA

I was shaking with frustration.

No no no I've been there. They're not there. Where else would she go?

You checked her profiles? You know how to do this, Finder

She's a denier. There's nothing.

Come on help me I need you need to mail this

I was shaking so bad the voice recognition was breaking down.

Help me. Please

I've always known the Librarian was human, and he came through for me.

Whoa Finder this lady is heavy shit. She's firewalled up the wazoo. No wonder even you couldn't break in. Who is she?

Some batty old lady.

Maybe not, Finder

He began spitting out a list of GPS coordinates. I saved them into a text file.

That's her last 30 days. Okay?

I owe you, buddy. Thanks.

Maybe you can take me to the beach sometime.

I'll do that.

I sorted the list of coordinates by frequency and started the lookup with 37.41704989999999, -122.14513310000001. Maxman had been there four times. It was 1001 Page Mill Road in Palo Alto. I knew it well. Adnomyx.

I considered the options. A tiny adhesive bomb just big enough to shatter a panel of Hyper Glass in Pellissier's living quarters to get me inside. A heavy-duty soporific in the air conditioning system. A big, old-fashioned gun. I liked the idea of causing harm. I loaded it all into a carrying case and booked an Uber for all day. I swallowed two OxyContin and chased them with some high-quality meth I'd gotten in payment for a job.

I was going to make Pellissier tell me where Maxman was, and then I'd make the old lady give me the Parrot. I had no doubt I was going to find the Parrot and bring him home.

On the ride into the Valley, I accessed the satellite maps and zoomed in on the Adnomyx complex. If I used the gun, I could just go in the main entrance, grab whoever was in the lobby or at the desk for a shield, and bully my way back to Pellissier's private apartment. If I used the gas, I'd have to skulk my way to the mechanicals wing—where I might need to use the gun anyway.

As I scoped it out, I found a hiking trail that ran from a residential road over wooded hills down to the back of the complex, where her living quarters snugged into the trees. I went for that, and the contact explosive. It would be quickest and get me closest to the Parrot.

I parked the Uber in front of a vintage ranch house, its picture windows protected by heavy drapes. A frizzled palm tree dozed in a bed of raked river stone. The street was silent, its residents at work or tucked away from the heat of the day.

The afternoon light was golden, belying the intensity of the sun. The air smelled of baked oak leaves.

I slung my carrier bag over one shoulder, missing the weight of the Parrot. *Soon*, I told myself, feeling the righteous anger build. I walked to the dead end of the street, slipped around the wooden fence marking the trailhead, and began to jog the four miles to Adnomyx. The thick air raked my lungs.

A half mile in, where oaks began to give way to eucalyptus, my mobile sounded. Thin Man.

"Not a good time," I said and swiped to end the call. Seconds later, he was back.

"I said, it's not a good time."

Thin Man was his usual tart self. "I need a report. Have you made any progress?"

"Oh, yes. Your friend was into some strange stuff."

There was a beat, and then, "I doubt that."

"Don't. I'm in the middle of something. I'll call you later." I cut the connection and set my mobile to ignore all incoming.

I reached the crest of the hill, where I could look down at Adnomyx and the spread of corporate campuses beyond it. Most of them were older, all odd angles and multiple levels, large expanses of windows retrofitted with metal awnings and Hyper Glass covers. You could tell the newer ones by the way they kept low to the ground, gathering most of the mass in the center, where it could be insulated from the heat. Adnomyx was one of the more elegant ones, carefully designed to minimize energy consumption by orienting itself to the north, windows carefully set like jewels.

I paused to organize my equipment. I unwrapped the contact bomb from its packaging, and set it on a rock. I slipped the Glock out of its holster and stuck it in the right pocket of my pants. I really wanted to shoot Maxman, but I had no plans to. Unlike property damage, shooting someone was an unfixable crime. I picked up the bomb, armed it, and cradled it in my left hand. Then I went down the hill at a run.

As I skidded down the last quarter mile where the path was steepest, I pulled the gun out of my pants and held it pointing down, safety on. The sight of the gun would shock them, then the concussion of the bomb would terrify them. I was hoping that the Parrot would realize that it was me, coming to save him.

As I rounded a travertine outcropping and slid onto flat ground, I almost ran into Pellissier. She was standing calmly in the shadow of the building, a few yards from a concrete deck and a decorative metal door painted citron.

"Our security system has been tracking you since you left Berkeley," she said. "I knew you'd be coming."

"That illegal behavioral database."

She shrugged. "It's useful." She looked at the gun and bomb in my hands without overt fear. "You don't need weapons. Your bird is safe."

My blood pressure surged, and sweat broke out on my body like a splash of cold rain. For a second, I thought I might lose consciousness, the relief was so intense.

"Where is he?" I choked it out.

She smiled, the delicate lips curving more. "He's right inside. We've been taking good care of him."

"Your friend, Roh Maxman, tried to kill me, and she stole the Parrot."

She sighed, and the courteous smile disappeared, but she didn't look that upset. "I'm very sorry. Please come in, and you'll see he's fine." She climbed to the deck and opened the yellow door. "Please."

I put the gun back in my pocket and paused to disarm the bomb and then followed her in. We were in a small vestibule, its floor paved with satiny granite tiles, the walls washed in a cooler tint of the door's yellow. A row of cabinets on the left-hand wall held more of the wooden curios. Through a door in the right-hand wall, I got another view of the living room where I'd been the last time. I followed her through the door and into the big room, my eyes immediately going to the couch along the back wall.

The Parrot was there, in the middle of the group, the dog in him clearly dominant. The boy held him in his lap, the Parrot's head resting in the bruised crook of one sticklike arm. He sprawled on his back, baring his belly to the stroking of the clones' clubby hands.

It took the Parrot a split second to catch my scent and another second to begin to wriggle away from the grasping, stroking hands, get onto his feet and then swoop into my arms.

A warm rush spread out from the center of my chest where I clasped him to me, flushing the last of the old lady's poison out of my pores. The Parrot snuffled contentedly into my armpit. He was glad to see me, but not at all traumatized.

It was only then that I noticed the old woman, sitting in a low armchair off to the side of the couch. She looked shocked. My rage came up again.

"You!" was all I could say. I took a step toward her.

Pellissier moved toward me. "Wait! Don't. Please." She looked at me. "Can you sit? Please?"

"I didn't hurt him," the boy piped up. "We took care of him."

"He's mine!" I gritted, outraged.

"He's not a possession. He's a living being," the old lady said querulously.

"You think I don't know that? I made him."

Pellissier stepped between us. "Mother, please."

That was enough of a jolt to make me stare.

"She's your mother?" I looked at the old lady, hunkered into her waterfall of hair. "But…people like you can't reproduce."

"You can say eugies. Go ahead. I don't mind."

I looked over at Pellissier, clutching the Parrot a little tighter to me. He *greeped* in protest; I relaxed my grip and stroked his head. "And how did the progeny of that wacko end up running a big-coin business? I don't believe this."

"That's not fair," Pellissier said. "Will you *please* sit down?"

I backed into one of the upholstered chairs, keeping a wary eye on the old lady. I didn't like the way she was looking at the Parrot. In the corner, the clones murmured to each other, stroking the boy now. It made my stomach turn to think about the Parrot entwined with them.

"I'm so sorry about your bird," Pellissier said again. "My mother didn't mean any harm."

"She poisoned me and took the only thing I…love," I said, the words sticking in my throat. It's not a word I use much. But that was surely what this feeling was.

"You don't know anything about love," the old lady piped up in a bitter voice. "You don't partake of the essence—"

"Mother, stop." Pellissier turned sad eyes on me. "She's very old. She doesn't think the way we do."

"There are drugs for that," I said.

She shook her head. "I wouldn't drug her. I'm not a member of the church, but I am my mother's daughter. In many ways."

"What does that mean? You believe in murder? Kidnapping?"

"No, of course not." She looked over at the boy—Cornell—who was stirring, disentangling himself from the groping, greedy paws. "But I believe in love and connection. Like she does. She's devoted her life to it."

I watched the old lady, muttering to herself, turning inside the cocoon of hair like an insect pupating. Not any vision of love that I could understand.

I couldn't see it. Pellissier ran one of the world's biggest corporations. She was known to be tough and a little cold. She'd have to be. And eugies were wired differently.

"Oh, so you believe in love?" It came out harsh and contemptuous, freighted with my anger.

She looked hurt, but she stood up to my anger. "I do," she said simply.

I just stared at her. At the end of the room, I could sense the slow shifting of Cornell and the clones. After a moment, she continued.

The boy Cornell made his way over to us, limping like it hurt him to walk. He looked more peaked and bruised than the last time I'd seen him. "Can I hold Pinkie again?" he asked me.

"What?"

"He means your bird," Pellissier said.

"We named him that," the boy said. "Because he's blue."

I clutched the Parrot tighter as I felt him stir and try to move toward the boy. I wasn't letting him go again.

"Please? Just for a minute?"

The Parrott stuck a claw into my thigh. He really wanted to get to the boy. So, I let go. He shoved off, flapped his wings once and landed in the little boy's waiting arms. Cornell smiled and curved his tiny body around the bird. He carefully lowered himself to the floor at our feet.

Pellissier looked down on him tenderly. "He has so little," she said.

"You can buy him anything he wants. Your mother, too. You could just buy them a bird each. You don't have to steal and murder to get what you want."

She shook her head. "My mother thought she was…rescuing your bird."

"She could have killed him."

"I know, I know. What can I say? She's going to be living with me now." She gave me a sidelong look but didn't accuse me of burning the old lady's house down. "I'll be able to take better care of her. And it never occurred to me that Cornell would like a pet. Or the Cousins."

"Pinky is special," the little boy said.

The old lady piped up again, "Anything you love is special."

Yeah, but the Parrot was truly special. I'd made him for me. I didn't say that, though. "Shut up," I told her.

"Be gentle with us," Pellissier said.

"Why should I?"

"Because we're human beings? Because we're dying?"

"We're all dying."

"Cornell and I are dying faster."

I looked for a sign in her face, her smooth skin, her delicate hands. I saw nothing.

"Yes," she said, "you can't see it on me. It's all inside. How much do you know about the New Eugenics?"

"Plenty."

"My mother was one of the first gene-edited babies. Her parents— my grandparents, although I haven't had much contact with them—wanted the best for their only child. But they were technical people; they didn't understand that nurturing—love—was the most important thing."

The delicate eyebrows drew together. I saw she was in pain, and wondered at it. I'd pegged her as a workaholic, spending day and night on the job. Where did this softness come from?

"My mother came out with all the desirable qualities—the beauty, extreme intelligence, physical stamina. They didn't know about the Freitak's and the other mutations. They showed up much later."

I looked at the old lady, trying to visualize her as young and beautiful. It was hard.

"She was also deeply emotional," Pellissier continued. "That was unexpected but it didn't seem like a problem. She took a deep breath, visibly collecting herself, and I saw the strong will take over from the softness.

"Then there was the social isolation, the fear and contempt for the eugies," she went on. "My mother grew up lonely and miserable. She so much wanted a child—much more than most women in those days. She was rich, a 1-percenter. She almost died from all the experimental procedures, but in the end, it worked. She had me."

I was impressed; in awe of the tech that must have been needed to create a viable germ cell from such an altered organism.

"Cloning?"

"Modified cloning. A cloning process with insertion of donor DNA so that the embryo—me—would be individuated."

"An illegal procedure."

"Yes."

"But available to those with enough money."

She shrugged delicately. "Yes. But we paid the price, ultimately. My mother's mind began to deteriorate decades ago. She has Freitak's lesions in her brain. I have them, too."

She bowed her head, as if showing me the sarcomas eating into her brain. I pictured this polished and powerful woman withering, withdrawing into a mumbling world of delusion. Despite her wealth and accomplishments, yes, I pitied her.

"What was it like for you? Being her child?" I tried hard to keep contempt out of my voice.

But she must have sensed it. She looked defiant. "My mother did her utmost best to give me what she never had—a mother's love. And she pretty much did. It wasn't easy." She looked over at her own child, tangled with the clones.

I stroked the Parrot. It was the same impulse, I realized.

"My mother did a lot of seeking. Drugs, gurus, neurosurgery. The Church was the end result."

I snorted.

"I know it looks crazy to outsiders, but there's something real going on inside. There's even a scientific basis for it. You're all about science, I suppose?"

"That's right."

"So, you know about oxytocin."

"Sure. I use it when necessary."

She sat back in her chair. I could see she was more comfortable talking about science than mother love herself.

"People have mostly forgotten that oxytocin is natural. It flows into us when we're intimate, when we connect with other people—in the real world. And that's what they're doing in the New Church."

I tuned into the little waves of calm coming into me as I fingered the Parrot's soft fur and feathers. Yes, she was right.

But they'd stolen him away from me.

"And that jibes with stealing the Parrot how?"

She softened again. It was fascinating to watch the shifts from control to gentleness. "I'm sorry. I'm sorry, I'm sorry, I'm sorry." I was shocked to see a tear wet her cheek. "The flaws in my mother's gene eventually showed. She's been in cognitive decline for several years. She got weirder, and the Church did too. I know there's no excuse, but I wish you could see…"

She flushed. "Do you blame me?"

I sighed. "No. I don't blame you. I'd do the same thing if I had the coins and a death sentence." I watched the Parrot, snuggled contentedly in the dying little boy's arms. Parrots live a very long time. "If your mother had her way, I'd be dead right now."

A flash of impatience. "But you're not."

"But you owe me."

"What do you want? You've got your bird back."

"Miraluna Rose. She came to your mother's church. Several times. I need to find her." I looked for a reaction from the old lady, but she was sunk into some reverie, stroking the Parrot's head where it rested on the boy's peaked chest.

The flush on Pellissier's face was strong enough to obliterate the tattoos around her eyes.

"That, I can't help you with."

"You mean, you won't." I looked menacingly at the old lady, and she was alert enough to let out a little squawk of alarm.

She looked anguished. "You don't know what you're asking."

"I'm doing a job, and I never fail."

"I won't help you. You're dark!"

The same thing her crazy mother had said to me. "I'm just doing a job," I repeated.

"I'll make a bargain with you," she said desperately.

"It's not about the money. It's about honor," I said. I stood up and took the Parrot out of the boy's arms. Both of them squeaked in protest but I didn't let go. "I can just make your mother tell me what I need to know." The Parrot squirmed in my arms. The boy scrambled back into the arms of the clones.

Pellissier stood up too. "Why don't you find things out about ReMe?" she said breathlessly. "That's where you should be looking."

"My employer is an investor in ReMe," I said, as much to test her as because I cared. "I don't shit in my own soup."

"Is that all you care about? Will you take any job, do anything to get paid?"

"I'm looking for a missing woman. She might be in danger."

"She is in danger! From you." She moved over to where her mother sat, brooding or nodding off, I wasn't sure. She put a hand on the old lady's shoulder. "My mother is a hero," she said. "She fought the corporations that said they owned our genes. I'll help her fight you, too."

I was bewildered. I dug my fingers into the Parrot's fur. "Fight me for what?"

She took a deep breath; I could see the way it calmed her. "You're so good at finding things. Find out about ReMe. Take a deep, hard look at what they're doing. Then come back to me. Tell me if you still want to find Miraluna Rose."

"Then will you tell me where she is?"

Pellissier sat down on the arm of her mother's chair and wrapped her arm around the old lady's shoulders. "Find out about ReMe. Then we'll talk."

* * *

75

I'm the Finder. It's what I do. Finding things for paying clients is a necessary part of my job, but getting paid isn't the motivation. There's pure joy in the hunt and the discovery, and part of the intrigue is finding the unexpected. Finding out can be as good as finding.

The job had shifted for me. It was a puzzle with many more pieces. I was still bitter at what the old lady had put me through. But I'd been affected by Pellissier's softness—and her explanation. I'd have to be careful that didn't cloud my thinking.

She'd given me an intriguing clue in ReMe. I'd follow it up and then decide if I still wanted to find Miraluna Rose.

The ReMe complex was out in Ceres, the suburban sprawl where big biotech companies go when they want protection from government snooping. I'd taken a single-person drone straight from Adnomyx, booking a sales appointment with ReMe on the trip. The drone landed on the complex's private air strip, set at the edge of a couple of acres of gravel.

It was ten degrees hotter than in Palo Alto. The hot sun grated off the gravel, and the Parrot shifted and panted. I took his hood out of my bag and put it on his head. The front is sunscreen mesh so he can still see and smell everything. It was the best solution I'd found for him.

Besides making the Parrot happy, the business with the hood let me palm a drone bee scout.

Little Googles waited to ferry visitors across the gravel to the building entrance, a smallish pop-out from the otherwise featureless metal walls of the factory itself. An angular steel sculpture had been plopped near the entrance in an unambitious attempt at place-making. I hopped a Google, moving the Parrot to my forearm, as the drone's autopilot sent it back toward the city. He *greeped*, glad to be back in air conditioning.

I held my mobile up to the reader at the door and it slid open. An interior door did the same, leading me into a utilitarian reception room. Three people stared into arrays of screens, busily swiping and murmuring into headsets. The man in the middle swiveled to face me. His elaborately spiked hairdo made him look like a quizzical marmoset. "Hello."

"I'm here for my three-thirty appointment."

He glanced and swiped. "Findhorn."

"That's right."

"An initial consultation, correct? Someone will be right with you."

Yes, I'm ridiculously old-fashioned. I use my real name as my social name. The Finder should have nothing to hide.

No sooner had he spoken than an inner door opened and another man stepped out, holding his mobile out toward me. I responded, holding my own out so we could beam. "I'm Davis Chang," he told me. He was wearing a modern take on the traditional men's suit, made of some buff-colored synthetic. The getup screamed "sales." I took off the Parrot's hood so he could get a better look at Chang in the subdued light, and the man eyed him dubiously. "We don't allow, uh, animals in here."

"It's a synthetic, licensed as a comfort bioid, as you can see in my beam." It wasn't a complete lie.

"Of course, no problem," he murmured. "Come this way." Neither Chang nor the receptionist noticed my drone bee take off as I shook out the hood before replacing it in my bag.

Chang led me down a short corridor to a private conference room. It was a small space just big enough to hold a round table, four chairs, and a bare credenza against one wall. No frills in this place—at least no visible frills. I'd have bet big coin that its surveillance and recording systems were government-level.

As we entered, Chang motioned me to a chair. I sat, placing the Parrot on the back of the chair next to me. Chang opened a drawer in the credenza and pulled out a large tablet, placing it on the table and sitting to face us. It sprang to life as he touched it, brighter than the room's recessed lighting, illuminating his face from below. "How can we help you?"

"I think it's time for me to think about physical preservation." That's the great thing about the new privacy system. I could tell him anything I wanted; all he'd be able to get from my public profile was my trust score, which was excellent. Later on, of course, with the right credentials—which I was sure ReMe had—he'd be able to see not only my public profile but the top level of my financials, and he'd know I wasn't the kind of elite they usually did business with. But my identity would hold for now.

"Do you have medical necessity?"

"Not yet. But I've been advised it's better to get this done before I need to."

"So true." He tapped information into his tablet. "We have three levels of service. The first level, RePosit, is simple tissue cloning and storage. We have a patented process that creates undifferentiated stem cells that can be banked until needed."

"What if I want a full clone?"

He sighed. "Clone is such an imprecise term, Findhorn. As soon as we harvest and process your cells, you could call the result a clone. But the other two levels are more advanced. Level two, ReGrow, takes those cloned stem cells and grows whatever kind of tissue you need—skin, a lung, a kidney. Any part of your body can be replaced with a bioidentical substitute."

"Then why would anyone need the full deal—the Absolutes that we've all seen in the media?"

Chang sat back and smiled. "Great question! And the answer is, you don't—not anymore. The full-body clones, the Absolutes, were actually an interim stage in the development of our product. Earlier on, we had no choice but to create an independently functioning organism with internal systems that could maintain itself and its components. But that was very wasteful."

I winced, thinking about the poor, used-up bodies, stripped of parts until they were no longer viable, and then euthanized.

"We've just announced the beta of our next iteration," he continued. "We're looking at a full release next year."

Chang touched his screen and turned it toward me so I could see the video that began to play. The ReMe logo sparkled and dissolved to a scene of a pristine laboratory where workers in full biohazard suits worked at long rows of tables. Through the screen's speaker, I heard, "ReMe's scientists have perfected the ability to regenerate the human body, eliminating disease and disability to allow *everyone* to live the life they deserve."

The scene shifted to an animated diagram showing cells twirling around a glowing box before descending into its interior. From the base of the box, a stream of identical pink tablets flowed. As they fell toward the bottom of the screen, they became flowers, individual, unique pink blossoms with a horrid resemblance to flesh.

"ReMe's innovative process for on-demand tissue creation allows greater flexibility than ever before," the narrator's voice proclaimed, "while reducing the expense associated with long-term storage of complicated organics. Just in time, just what you need." The visual switched to an overhead shot of the ReMe factory, zooming further out until it was the earth seen from space, as the narrator concluded triumphantly, "Your own new, healthy tissue is ready when *you* need it. More health, more life. Regeneration. ReMe!"

I nodded. "Very impressive."

Chang looked smug. "Streamlining the process will let us roll it out faster, to more people." He switched expressions like a news host shifting from the latest biotragedy to a heart-warmer. "Now, in regard to your own regenerative needs, many people begin the ReMe relationship with a simple RePosit. If you have no known medical issues, that may be adequate for your current health status. If you do have any known pathologies, we should discuss beginning immediately with level two, ReGrow. A heart or a kidney, for example, takes time to develop, and to be honest, there are sometimes failures in the process."

I had an unpleasant image of dog food, and ran my hand over the Parrot's back, letting the familiar softness of his fur wipe it away. "Level one will be fine," I said. "How much is it going to cost?"

Chang changed his expression to serene. It was as though he was swiping them across his face. "If you'll allow me to take a few biometric measurements right now, we'll create a custom proposal for you."

"Why do you need to do that? Isn't the process the same for everyone?"

Chang waved his hand airily. "Oh, you know. DNA. Epigenetics. All that sort of stuff. It's more complicated than most people think. *You* must know that," he added confidentially, with a nod to the Parrot. The Parrot *greeped* back at him.

"Let me think about it. I'll get back to you," I said. Chang's smile became bitterly polite. "Of course."

* * *

As I walked across the lobby, I took out my mobile, as people always do, and recalled the drone. It landed unobtrusively on my sleeve. I knew it hadn't been picked up by ReMe's security system. It's 60 percent pure *Apis mellifera*, and its mass and infrared profile are almost identical to a real insect's. Even in the desert of the Central Valley, there are still insects. The drone has very little onboard electronics; most of the data it generates is transmitted immediately to my private cloud where it's stored and analyzed, so it doesn't need bulky storage.

After me and the Parrot had boarded another private drone back to Berkeley, I logged onto my cloud servers to see what the bee had given me. By navigating the corridors and whatever rooms it could gain entry to, either through open doors, cracks, or the ventilation system, it had created a basic topographic map. By itself, the rudimentary map didn't tell me much, but it would inform the Parrot's visit—and the Parrot would be loaded.

* * *

The next night, we were back. We'd done it the slow, roundabout and highly secure way: Public drone from Berkeley to Modesto; anonymized Uber to Ceres proper; and then another private vehicle from a very select, secure and high-priced service I subscribe to. I directed it to park on a hill half a mile from the ReMe factory. A thin, chill wind ruffled the fronds of eucalyptus trees around us, and my footsteps stirred up the old-man scent of their fallen leaves.

I asked the Parrot to hop up onto an outcropping of granite and began to set him up. I fitted his carbon-fiber harness over his neck, carefully threading the straps under his wings. Then, I began to attach his electronics. He could turn on his stereo infrared camera by tapping a switch above his right wing. Yes, the Parrot is that smart. In fact, much, much smarter. The camera and sensors would feed data into a memory chip in his rig; trying to transmit that much data over the air would doubtless set off the security system.

I knew he could get inside. The bee had identified two possible entry points. One, an emission stack that was improperly covered, was dangerous.

He'd need to read the atmospheric sensor attached to his chest—the bird part of him was super-sensitive to air quality.

The second possible entry point would take a little social engineering—something the dog part of him was excellent at. It was a guard's office next to a loading dock on the north side. The office didn't connect directly to the factory, but there was a simple ventilation grate in the ceiling, something the Parrot could easily handle with his beak. If he could get the guard to come out of the office and out onto the loading dock, he could slip back in with him. The Parrot is equally good at slinking along the floor like a dog and flying soundlessly up above. People indoors almost never look up above eye level. As long as he flew quietly, he'd be good.

Some people think a parrot's shriek sounds like a baby being tortured. That would be the diversion for the guard.

When he was all loaded up, I looked him in the eye. We both knew how dangerous this was. If he got trapped inside the building, he had one weapon besides his speed and intelligence. The stink bomb. The stink bomb was my custom mix of chemicals and pheromones designed to create physiological and emotional panic, and the chems were backed up with a subsonic siren that makes humans feel like their insides are turning to mush. The chemical blast would last only 17 seconds, hopefully long enough to let the Parrot shoot for the exit.

I rubbed the bare spots below his ears and then gave the vestigial flaps a little tug.

"Okay, buddy. Have fun out there." The Parrot enjoys a bit of bravado. But I was worried, sure. The only communication we'd have was a small GPS transmitter that would let me plot his location against the map the bee had generated.

* * *

We'd planned the Parrot's spy mission to last no more than twenty-two minutes. Longer than that and muscle fatigue from all the extra weight he was carrying would set in. At sixteen minutes, I began to sweat, watching the dot of his position moving in the interior of the building. At 18:03, the dot began moving fast toward the main entrance, and then I heard alarms ring out from the complex, the shrill bells arrowing through the night air. The ReMe complex lit up like a city street, and as I watched through my infrared sight, I saw bodies swarm out of the main entrance and a couple of doors along the side of the building. Then, on my GPS screen, I saw the Parrot's dot zooming away in a straight line toward where I waited on the hill.

He didn't make it. The dot began to move erratically, slowed, dipped and stopped. I began to run down the hill.

I found him lying in a tangle, one wing stretched out at an unnatural angle. His fur was matted with foxtails, clumps of feathers among the clods of dirt. But he was alive.

I put one hand on his chest to support him while I carefully worked the harness off him. He whined when I had to move his outstretched wing and then looked trustingly into my face to reassure me. I sat down in the dirt, cradling him against me and cried.

"I'm sorry, baby. I'm so, so sorry."

You know the stakes, you know the danger, but when you see your best friend broken like that, it's worse than you can imagine. I took off my jacket and wrapped him up snugly so that he wouldn't be jostled too much when I carried him back to the Uber. I was so distraught that I almost forgot to grab his harness.

* * *

Back at the warehouse, I injected the Parrot with morphine sulfate, then gave him a subcutaneous injection of B-12, and an intravenous dose of oxytocin. He whined when I spread out his wing to scan it and then nuzzled my fingers with his beak to let me know it was okay. There was soft-tissue damage at his shoulder but nothing broken. He'd run and fly again. I wrapped his wing tight against his chest and watched him until he fell asleep.

I dropped 1500 milligrams of aniracetam to amp up, and then I uploaded his footage to my cloud servers. I used a 3D modeling program backed by AI to automatically fill in the topography of ReMe headquarters that he'd flown over. My brave, tenacious partner had covered a lot of ground. I had a video wireframe of most of the complex. The modeling program estimated colors and surfaces based on a master government database of infrared signatures I'd hacked into a while back. It couldn't do things like showing what was on a screen or picking up lettering on machinery, but within an hour I had a virtual reality landscape.

I grabbed an iced bottle of NeuroFocus, popped some liposomal phenyl-GABA and put on my VR headset, setting the motion speed to flythrough. I moved quickly past the front office, flying through corridors of office space where employees worked at screens. The modeling of the people wasn't too exact; I could see hair styles and body sizes and shapes, even the colors of the clothing, but all of it schematically. I slowed down when I passed through a changing area that led to a decontamination room hung with empty suits. Beyond was a vast factory space with lines of vats ringed by rows of lab tables. Workers moved through the area carefully, encumbered by their protective suits.

It was much bigger than I'd expected. ReMe's business must be booming.

At the far side of the factory floor was a short corridor with positive airflow pushing back into it. I could see how the Parrot had slowed down as he flew through. In VR, it didn't slow me down at all.

The next chamber looked like an indoor greenhouse—a greenhouse growing people. Several acres of white-tiled floor space held rows of glassed-in structures, each the size of an old-fashioned bungalow. I swooped closer and hovered over one.

It contained twelve glass trays on stands about waist-height, each about as big as a child's bed. Each tray was filled with clear, straw-colored liquid that came from a spray nozzle that traveled back and forth above the bed, keeping it constantly moist. The modeling program hadn't done a great job on what was in the trays, but I could see enough. Each held a pinkish mass about the size of a human torso, fetal and undifferentiated except for four knobs along the sides and one larger knob on top.

I flew further along the rows. The farther they were from the entrance, the more the knobs elongated or rounded out, pushing out into rudimentary heads and limbs. I saw one squirm, and my stomach squirmed in response.

This was no level two. Despite what Chang had said, ReMe was growing full-blown clones, the Absolutes he'd said were no longer necessary. And hundreds of them.

I paused the flythrough and took off the VR helmet, keeping my eyes closed for a moment to adjust. I went over to the Parrot. He was sleeping deeply, occasionally making little chuckling noises in the back of his throat. I grabbed a container of chicken-flavored Soylent out of the fridge, poured a glass and drank it down. Then I went back to the VR. The VR status bar told me I was barely halfway through the flythrough.

I lay back on the couch, put the helmet back on, and tilted my head to resume. I flew over the rest of the glass houses to the back, where a wall of translucent glass was broken by a set of heavy glass double doors. One was half open, and a worker was part of the way through. That's how the Parrot had gained entrance. I followed his path and flew into a nightmare.

A sea of deformed, lumpy bodies surged back and forth in an almost-empty room. They were naked except for a thin band around each one's neck. They shambled and stumbled, bouncing against each other as they milled around. They were for the most part pitifully misshapen. Although almost all had the club feet and stumpy hands typical of the Absolutes, many of their bodies had unnatural hollows traced by ugly scars. A missing breast or a sunken chest evidenced the flesh they had donated to their primaries.

The central floor space held one long metal trough that was filled with a thick brown substance. Absolutes stumbled up to it and dipped their hands in, bringing the brown glop to their mouths, licking it off the stubs of their hands while the ones behind them pushed up against them, trying to get to the trough. As each Absolute finished and turned away, another edged in to take its place.

Along the walls, sated Absolutes lolled on plastic pads, sometimes nuzzling each other or licking away the traces of food on faces and hands. Pellissier had said it was horrible. That wasn't even close. It was a warehouse of destroyed bodies.

I really didn't want to go any further, but the readout said I still had 15 percent of the model to go. And the Parrot had risked his life to get it for me. I flew quickly over the teeming bodies, trying to see them as nothing more than masses, heading through another translucent glass wall at the far end. I passed through another decon chamber with the same row of empty hazmat suits hanging like ghouls in a crypt.

The final room was much smaller, no more than a couple thousand square feet. The walls were lined with neatly organized lab benches and racks of electronic equipment. I recognized cell culture hoods, cryonic storage and incubators, all top of the line, as well as the usual clutter of pipettes, flasks, cell counters, and microscopes. There was plenty I didn't recognize, but then, I'm an amateur.

In the center of the room were seven stainless steel pods, studded with dials and knobs and penetrated by stainless steel tubes, each big enough for a man to lie down in. A curved piece of glass was inset into the top of each pod, so I dropped down to the closest one and looked in.

The pod held a woman—a wondrously strange and strangely beautiful woman. She seemed to be sleeping. Masses of orange hair pillowed her head, and there was light orange down on her chest. Her eyes were closed but I could see that they were a little closer together than normal. Her skin was very pale, almost white, but her lips and nipples were chocolate brown. I could see the tip of one ear nestled into the orange hair; it didn't have an earlobe. The whole effect was off enough to be intriguing without being uncanny. This was no Absolute.

I peered into another pod. It also held a sleeping woman. Her scalp, arms and chest were covered with what looked like downy white feathers, softly transitioning into creamy skin. My IRL fingers twitched. I ached to touch her.

The next pod held still another woman, this one with skin a deep cobalt blue. Her head was hairless and earless. She had no eyebrows or eyelashes. Her lips were thin and iridescent gold. Her cobalt breasts and belly were marked with thin lines of gold. I could see her chest expanding and contracting as she breathed, the golden tracings moving apart and coming together.

Each pod held a different woman, monstrous and gorgeous. I was looking at a chimera factory.

I pulled off the VR headset and lay back in my recliner. I pulled my breath deep into my belly and then let it seep out in a long sigh. I thought about science. I thought about making things because you wanted to. Then I got up to check on the Parrot.

He was sleeping peacefully, hunkered down on all fours, his claws grasping into the cushion for balance. I ran a gentle finger along the little feathery crest on his head and down his back into the line of soft blue fur. I scratched his back between his wings and he *wuffled* in pleasure.

I loved the Parrot. He was beautiful and unique among all creatures. I knew he loved me. I'd never thought to wonder whether he was happy being what he was. Would he rather be all dog, taking walks on a leash so he could smell the bushes? Would he rather be a bird, flying the heat-shimmering skies searching for clean water? Was I selfish?

Yes, of course I was. We are what we are. Me and the Parrot both. And the Parrot wouldn't have been a bird or a dog instead. He'd have been nothing. That's what I told myself.

Then I thought about what was behind that series of doors at ReMe. What would a snake woman want from life? What kind of life was she being born into?

I went back to the big screen and booted up the security footage from Thin Man's mansion. I scanned through it until I found the spot where Miraluna Rose in her tiny dress was just turning back from looking at herself in her mirror. I grabbed a still. I loaded it into a computer vision program and used it to magnify the image, the computer algorithm filling in detail as it zoomed, until I could see her clearly.

Clearly enough to see the subtle strangeness in her face. Her eyes were slightly too big and too far apart. That self-satisfied perpetual smile was caused by an overly full upper lip that pushed her mouth forward into just the suggestion of a muzzle. Her eyes were the impossible blue-green of sea ice, and I saw the bloom of iridescence gleaming on her skin. I realized her sea-green hair wasn't dyed; it sparkled with myriad colors like sun-dazzled water. She was inhumanly attractive, impossibly lovely. Someone's dream of a Venus birthed from the ocean and the jungle.

ReMe had made her. I was supposed to find her and bring her back. I knew now I'd never give her back to Thin Man. But I was still caught up in the mystery. I was a finder, and I needed to know more.

I thought about the women from the spa with their fantastical decorations. I'd assumed they'd had extreme body modifications, but when I compared them in my mind's eye with the creatures I'd seen in the ReMe footage, I thought I recognized the same fiendishly playful meddling with the human genome.

I needed to go back to Las Aromas.

I prepared an IV drip for the Parrot, saline and glucose to boost the healing process. I injected a bit more morphine and then carefully inserted the IV needle into the jugular vein. While I was at it, I set up an ozone IV for myself. Then I pulled a big glass of water from the recycler, scooped some brown rice from the cooker into a bowl, and sprinkled cricket powder on top. I put the food on the table in front of the couch, hung the IV from the standing lamp next to it, sat down and slipped the needle into my port. Then I sat back and ate, mindfully and gratefully, while the ozone did its work.

A half hour later, I was revitalized and ready to face the trip. The Parrot stirred when I touched him. His eyes looked less sunken and his nasal mucosa was pink and healthy. As I stroked him, he settled into a more relaxed position and let out little *snurkles*. He was going to be okay. I clipped a biomonitor to his uninjured wing and synced it to a monitoring app on my mobile.

"I love you," I told him. Weird, I'd never said that to him and now I found myself saying it a lot. Whatever.

I dressed in a loose-fitting suit I'd had made when I was doing corporate work. It had extra pockets for electronics and a built-in battery for juggling a bunch of multimedia recorders. I wasn't planning on using any electronics, but I thought the suit made me look like a 1-percenter.

I got a Google to the public transportation hub and a regular commute jet to Laxangeles, then hopped an Uber to Las Aromas. The outside was as clean and discreet as the last time. No one was going in or coming out.

The inside was as cool and pink as before. The same jellyfish bobbed serenely in the aquarium on the back wall. A different woman was behind the desk. She was wearing a stylish white dress cut to show off a long neck and muscular shoulders. Her skin was a glossy chestnut brown; a wave of thick black hair with a single white streak sprang from the top of her head, falling straight down her shoulders. Her round eyes were deep brown and fringed with extremely long lashes. She was almost conventionally beautiful; there was in her that same uncanny thing that made her beauty disturbing. As she looked at me, I saw a quiver run down the skin of her shoulders and arms. Now that I knew, her lineage was obvious.

When she didn't speak, I said, "Is Deirdre here?"

She quivered again. "What do you want?" Her voice was low and sweet.

"I want a massage. From Deirdre." I proffered my mobile.

She ignored it. "Deirdre is booked up today."

I sighed. "I'll pay an extra five coins to bump her next appointment."

"I can't do that."

I leaned toward her across the counter and put some menace into my voice. "What can you do for me?"

She shied away. "Deirdre isn't available," she said again.

"What about you then?"

"No," she said breathlessly. "What do you want?"

"I want to see Deirdre."

"You can't."

"If she's busy, I'll wait until she gets off work and talk to her then."

She darted her eyes, panicky. "No. You can't."

"Why not? What time does she get off?"

She didn't answer, just tossed her head around as though she was looking for a way to escape.

I was relentless. "She has to go home sometime, right? She has to eat. I want to buy her a meal."

"No," she moaned.

"What? She doesn't go home? She doesn't eat?"

"I don't know."

"Listen. I don't want to make trouble. Can you give her my info and ask her to call me?"

"We're not supposed to." She glanced up at the ceiling.

"Let me book an appointment for next week then. Can I do that?"

"She's—"

"What? She's booked all through next week? How about the week after?"

She tossed her head helplessly, her skin aquiver.

I leaned toward her and lowered my voice to a whisper. "It's about Miraluna Rose. I want to help her." The tawny woman gave a little whinny of fear and the quivering turned to shudders. "Maybe you need help, too."

The whites showed all around her black eyes. I thought she was going to pass out. "It's okay," I said helplessly. "Hey, it's okay." I began backing toward the door. "I'm leaving, okay? I'm leaving. Just…remember what I said."

* * *

I wanted to get back to the Parrot. I felt shaky, so I inhaled some oxytocin and then hopped a jet home. He was lying comfortably on his side, breathing easy. I ran my hand down his chest and he dug the top of his head into my palm. I gently unwrapped his wing and tested it with a finger. He was a little protective of it, but I didn't sense any pain. I gave him another injection of stem cells and made him a little dish of meal worms, yeast, and seaweed.

I sat on the couch and watched him eat. He was hungry; he's usually picky about the seaweed even though it's so good for him. I thought about rich nutrients traveling through his bloodstream, mending tendons. I flashed on having him at Las Aromas. What would he make of the wild hybrid smells? Would he let a horse woman cradle him in her arms?

I thought about the scientists at ReMe, making strange dreams into real women. I thought about Pellissier's clones. She called them the Cousins. They were imperfect and ugly. Necessary, but ugly.

It made me see the Parrot differently. The Parrot was necessary to me and beautiful. At least, I thought he was beautiful. Maybe Pellissier thought her clones were beautiful, too.

Was I any different from ReMe? Was the Parrot paying some price I didn't understand?

This was getting me nowhere. But somehow, I thought that if I could find Miraluna Rose, I might understand.

I messaged Thin Man. He came on through VirChat, looking sour. "I see you've been busy," he sneered, "but you haven't made any progress on finding Miraluna Rose."

"You've been tracking me?"

"Of course."

I shrugged. "Searches go where they lead me."

"You're paid to be leading *me* to *her*."

He was right; from his point of view, I was getting nowhere with the finding. A bigger problem was, I no longer had any interest in his point of view. I shrugged again. "Since you're not satisfied with my work, let's end the engagement. I'll return half of what you've paid me."

He sputtered. I could almost feel the waves of testosterone coming off him. "You've had access to private data about me and my partner. You can't just walk away."

The more agitated he became, the less engaged I was. Maybe it was residual calm from the oxytocin. I shrugged yet again. "I'm still bound by the non-D."

"You're bound to me by your word when you took the job."

I had every right to say that I hadn't known what he was asking when I took the job—or what Miraluna Rose was. But he probably didn't know about our foray into ReMe, and I didn't want him to. I wasn't sure where I was going with all this yet. And I still wanted to find Miraluna Rose. I decided it was better to string him along instead of inciting him to go after me with his very considerable resources.

The Parrot was done eating. He'd have to shit soon. And I didn't want him moving around too much. I needed to end the call. "You can't have it both ways," I told Thin Man, aka BruceWayne, aka Diverdown47. "Either I'm not doing a good job, or you want me to keep looking—but it has to be my way."

"I want you to get me the results I'm paying you for."

I could just see him in the board room, testing wills with the other big boys. "I'll do it my way." I closed the app before he could answer. I hadn't asked him anything about ReMe. He wouldn't have told me anything useful, and I already knew way more than he wanted me to.

I gathered the Parrot in my arms. It was good to feel him there. I took him up to the roof and put him down so he could shit. He lifted his head and snuffed the air, then began nosing around to find the right spot. I tasted the breeze myself. Berkeley air is unique. They say the Black Zone is inert but I swear it gives the air an extra tang that combines with the sting of the patchy eucalyptus groves and the ozone from thousands of electric Googles to create a perfume like nothing else.

I looked carefully to make sure there was no blood in the Parrot's shit. It looked good, just like it always looked. He was walking okay, too, holding his wings almost equally balanced. Warmth coalesced in my chest and flowed down into my belly. He was okay.

There are times when the right thing to do is nothing. We stood out there on the roof, the Parrot and me, and watched the gray sky turn gray-green. The windows of the buildings on the ridge flashed with the dying light and then brightened again as the LEDs came on inside them.

Then I took him back downstairs, put him on my bed and started my sleep stack. I lay down and put him on my chest, where he settled into a warm lump. It was like holding onto an energy source whose rays trickled into my bones. I let Miraluna Rose tumble around in the part of my brain that doesn't think, and fell asleep.

CHAPTER 10

I woke with a thick web of dreams clogging my mouth. The Parrot was next to me, stretched out on his side against my thigh. It felt good. Why hadn't I slept with him before? I reached down and tickled his chest feathers.

"Time to get to work," I told him.

I changed out his water and put out a dish of tofu and cricket powder for him, and then put my own share in the blender. I injected myself, dropped my meds, and drank the rest of the water from the recycler. I took two quick slugs of breakfast, sat down at the big screen, and pinged Pellissier.

This time I got right through; she'd put me on her white list. She was at a desk, a wall of screens next to her, a bank of windows to her right. Office.

She took one look at my face and said, "You saw."

"I saw."

"Do you still want to find Miraluna Rose?"

I still did. Just, not for Thin Man. "I don't know."

She leaned into the screen. "Do you think it's okay?"

"What?"

"Playing with life? Creating beings to be sold as slaves?"

Behind me, I heard the Parrot finishing off the last of his breakfast, making little sounds of satisfaction. Was he really just my slave?

I put Pellissier's feed up on the large screen, so I could see the nuances of her expressions. Not as good as being meat-to-meat, but good. "That doesn't bother you when it comes to the clones."

Rose flushed her chest. She looked anguished. "I didn't know. I was desperate. I'd have done anything to try to save Cornell. I still would." She looked away, looking into the past. "I didn't understand what they'd be like."

I could see it, see the way it tortured her. She went on. "When they're selling it to you, they talk about cloning in terms of tissue. The stem cells and platelets they could harvest for him. I didn't realize." She trailed off.

I felt bad for making her feel bad. And because I knew it gave me an advantage that I was going to use. "So, then you felt bad about Miraluna Rose, too."

She leaned back, her fingers toying with a small stone on the work table. "I didn't even realize what she was at first," she said. For the leader of a global corporation, there was a lot she seemed not to have realized. "I thought she was just very stylish. Then she asked for my help."

"Why did she come to you?"

"They're called ArcoTypes, did you know that? That's the brand name."

"There's a brand? They can't be selling them. It's not legal to even make them." A brand name for synthetic women mixed with wildness. No, it wasn't right.

"But they are." She looked straight at me, and I saw the drive and passion that must have made her a good CEO.

"So Miraluna Rose came to you. Was she already planning to run?"

She shifted on her chair, slipping off her sandals and tucking her feet under her. "At first, it was just for understanding."

"What?"

"She was trying to understand herself. Her place in the world."

Her place in the world. Miraluna Rose was a product. She was a product purchased by a very rich man who didn't know quite what to do with her. But she wanted more. Like Roh Maxman did.

"Why you?"

"We used to talk. At first, at parties at BruceWayne's house. Later, with VirChat. I'm probably the only person who treated her like a real person."

"What did you tell her?"

Pellissier gave a little shrug. "I tried to buy her, you know. It would have been the simplest way. But…BruceWayne wouldn't sell—not at any price."

"That must have made her crazy."

Pellissier looked out at the landscape beyond the darkened windows of her office, where the sun sizzled against tough yucca leaves. "She's…pragmatic. There's a sort of untouchable part of her that's above all this."

Cat, I thought. "So BruceWayne wouldn't sell," I said, to keep her talking.

"I offered her the only thing I had that could help her. Money. I set up a small nonprofit—the Maxman Institute."

I snorted.

She gave me a severe look. "I know what you think of my mother, and I don't entirely blame you. But before she…deteriorated, she was a revolutionary. They tried to strip the GEIVs of human rights, did you know that?"

"Yeah, I remember. When the Party of America First came into power."

"She was one of the lead plaintiffs in the class action suit. She was twelve years old."

That had been before cloning, but the hatred of the eugies was still intense. No wonder the old lady was crazy. That and the Freitak's eating her brain cells. I nodded respectfully. "So you set up the Institute?"

"I endowed it, and every month, I put enough coins in an operational account. When the time is right, we can litigate." Her voice had softened as she contemplated the past and her family history. I saw the little jolt as she remembered who she was talking to. She sat up straight. "The point is, ReMe needs to be stopped."

I'd already made my decision about Miraluna Rose. I wasn't going to return her to that desiccated house and the joyless man that inhabited it. "I'm not going after Miraluna Rose. But I'm not tangling with ReMe, either."

Even as I said it, I knew it wasn't true. I may work outside the law, but not outside of what's right. My adrenaline began to surge. Pellissier was correct. ReMe needed to be stopped.

I didn't get a chance to tell her I'd changed my mind, because my alarm began to shrill. The Parrot squawked and flew awkwardly around the room as something thumped against the front door. The front-door camera feed showed a person-sized mass wrapped in a shapeless hooded coat hurling itself against the door, over and over.

I cut the call with Pellissier and picked up my laser with my right hand, holding my left up in the air. The Parrot hopped to my shoulder, still squawking and fussing. He knows better, but the alarm sound is designed to resonate in the fear center. It works on us, too.

I opened the door, and the human lump fell through it and lay motionless on the floor. I cut the alarm and bent down, pulling aside the hood. It was Deirdre from Las Aromas.

A badly battered Deirdre. The naturally swollen lips were split, bruises were spreading out from the black rings around her eyes. The opalescent scalp was coated with dried blood.

The Parrot *greeped* in sympathy. I let him down onto the back of the couch and then bent to pick the woman up. I carried her to the couch and gently took her arms out of the coat, which was also damp with blood. She was still wearing the silky shift, now spattered dark.

I went to my med kit and got supplies, then began to clean her, starting with her face and scalp, gently sponging away the blood. I worked my down her body, going over all of the lustrous skin, the green nipples, skirting the naked green pubis. There were abrasions and bruises everywhere, but no major wounds. I coated the scrapes with ointment and bandaged the cuts, then covered her with a clean sheet. Through it all, she moaned but didn't open her eyes.

I called Pellissier back, flagging it as urgent. She answered immediately, looking concerned. "What was that about?"

"One of your ArcoTypes just landed on the floor of my warehouse." I spun the camera so she could see Deirdre lying on the couch, and Pellissier gasped. "Do you know her?"

"I don't think so. I can't be sure."

"She works at Las Aromas. Ever been there?"

She sneered. "Of course not. It's a fancy brothel for the venture capital boys."

A brothel. So the lack of daytime customers and the big bed in the treatment room made sense. "You're the patron saint of ArcoTypes. Any ideas on what to do with her?"

"Take her to the Institute. I'm sending you the address now. Ask for Jane Dobarro."

As I cut the call, I heard Deirdre moan again. The Parrot was perched on the back of the couch, delicately huffing her scent. Her eyes were open. "They did too much," she whispered.

"Shush," I said. "You're going to be okay."

CHAPTER 11

The Maxman Institute address Pellissier messaged me was one of the places Miraluna Rose had visited before she disappeared. It was way out in Palm Springs. While I was helping Deirdre get dressed in one of my shirts, which was about as long on her as the uniform she usually wore, a voice call came in on my mobile. It was the Librarian.

"Dude," I said automatically. "I didn't know you could call out."

"Yeah, getting better every day," he said. "But man, this is urgent. You got a drone on you."

I was feeding Deirdre some yeast broth. "There's always some drone on me."

"No, this is serious shit, man. Military-style stealth on this bugger. You wouldn't even see it."

Thin Man? Or Nihelroush? "So how'd you pick it up?"

"I've got a new gig," he said. "Tapped into the Internet of Things. I'm getting data from sensors all over the world."

Deirdre had finished the soup. We had to get out of there. "Rock on, dude. But I've got to move."

"I know it. Just, eyes on, okay?"

"Will do."

"Catch up later. At the beach?"

"You got it."

I didn't want to take Deirdre on public transportation. I assumed Thin Man knew all about Pellissier, the Maxman Institute and her bleeding-heart plans. But I didn't want him to connect me with Pellissier. And I didn't want Nihelroush to get Deirdre back.

That drone the Librarian had warned me about would have infrared strong enough to pick up our heat signatures inside the house, plus a night-vision video camera. Spoofing it would take precious minutes.

I have a few simple humanoid, battery-powered robots with heating elements that I use to mimic human heat signatures. I went to my storeroom and pulled out three: big, medium, and tiny. I set the medium and tiny one on the couch, next to Deirdre and the Parrot. Deirdre was still pretty out of it. "Help me," she pleaded when I placed the robot next to her.

"I'll help you," I said.

I called the Librarian back. He sounded excited. "Finder! Wut up?"

"Can you, by any chance, see the feed from this drone above my warehouse."

"Absolutely."

"Holy shit. I'm not even going to ask. Does the feed go both ways?"

"Finder, you're too much. It's a *camera*. Duh. No."

Of course not. Adrenaline was clouding my thinking. I'd need to be careful. And take something. "Can you maybe intercept the feed or break the transmission for a few seconds?"

"That's pretty intense. It's a whole network of nodes that go in all directions. No telling where the data is going. I'd have to find the hub." The lag was almost infinitesimal. "Got it."

"In three minutes, I'll signal you. If you can break the transmission for thirty seconds, I can get clear of the drone."

"You got it. I just set up a direct secured connection to me from your mobile."

"I hope you don't get wiped, my friend."

"Oh, they couldn't do that now."

I shook my head. "Librarian, you're something else."

He laughed. "Rockin' out with my cock out, man."

I cut the call.

I began a three-minute countdown in my head. I took an ampule of dex from the fridge and injected 15 mg, then took a big slug of water. I glanced over at Deirdre, wondering if I should give her a jolt. She was slumped a little sideways on the couch, but her eyes were open. The Parrot was nestled in her lap and she was stroking his head absently.

"What, now you're a lapdog?" I said. But actually, their position would make things easier. Two-point-five minutes.

I dragged two cold suits out of the locker. They were prototypes of extravehicular suits with internal refrigeration units designed for Mars colonists that I'd gotten off eBay. They'd briefly chill our bodies below the range of the drone's heat sensors.

I got everything into place. I arranged two of the robots more carefully on the couch, small one on top of the medium one with the large one, my doppelganger, on the armchair nearby. Then I picked up one of the cold suits.

"Deirdre. Deirdre, I need you to help me, okay?"

She looked at me blearily and nodded. This was no good. Two minutes. I went back to the fridge, prepared a needle with .5 mg of dex and jolted her. No time for subtle calculations—or to worry about how the dex would affect the nonhuman parts of her. Her eyes opened wide, she jerked, and her legs began to move rhythmically. Better.

I helped her get the cold suit on and zipped it up around her and the Parrot. "Hold on, buddy," I told him. I put them right on top of the medium robot.

I took my mobile out of my pocket, shrugged into my own cold suit, zipped up and lowered myself on top of the large robot. I used my home control app to blast the heating unit. The temperature zoomed up to eighty-five, ninety, ninety-five.

The idea was to briefly confuse the drone's infrared sensors. While they adjusted to the new ambient temperature, I'd lower the temperature in the cold suits, and the heated robots would take our place in the heat signatures. By the time the drone's sensors got back up to speed, they'd pick up only the robots. As we chilled and the robots heated simultaneously, the drone would transmit the robots' heat signatures instead of ours as we moved away.

I reached over and activated Deirdre's cold suit, hit my own switch, and then turned on the robots' heating elements. I reversed the house thermostat, then touched the Librarian's contact icon.

Go, go, go.

I dragged the Deirdre-Parrot package off the couch and out the door. I couldn't see or hear the drone, but I wouldn't. I rushed them a few yards down the street to a waiting Google and used one of my fake personas to send it toward the suburbs. I threw off my cold suit and worked Deirdre's off. Her injuries were still making her limp while the dex was making her muscles contract. Not a great combination, but at least she was upright. She and the Parrot were both shivering. I put my arm out so he could get back on my shoulder and warm up.

I canceled the Google's trip a quarter mile from the warehouse. We set down in the suburbs where the flat West Berkeley streets merge into North Oakland. I put my arm around Deirdre and supported her, walking slowly toward San Pablo until another empty Google purred past. We hopped it, and I gave it the address of the Hotel Mac in Point Richmond.

My mobile buzzed with an unknown caller. I swiped. It was the Librarian.

"Dude, we did it. You da man."

I couldn't help but smile. Always the elderly slang. "What's the drone doing?"

"Oh, it knows you're gone now. Took it a couple of minutes. One hundred seventy-two-point-nine seconds, to be exact. It's circling the area."

"Thanks, my friend. But, hey, you probably shouldn't be calling me."

The Librarian laughed. "No problemo. I'm connecting through a citizen's smart home network, by way of their toaster. Untraceable."

I had to laugh too. "Stay cool, man."

In Point Richmond, we switched to a private, secure Google and began the long trip to Palm Springs.

* * *

I got Deirdre settled on the bench seat across from me. She was shivering but looking more alert. I could feel the Parrot on my shoulder, quivering. "Go ahead," I told him. He hopped across and nestled in her lap. She could use his body heat. "What happened to you?" I asked.

She shivered harder; or maybe it was a shudder. "They did too much."

"What do you mean? Who?"

"It was a play party."

My stomach turned and then adrenaline heat flashed my skin. Some play. I tried to gentle my voice. "Does that happen a lot?"

Her eyes welled, and tears flowed down her cheeks. "Yes." It was a whisper.

"The other women, too?"

She gasped but didn't answer.

"It's over," I told her. "I promise. I'm taking you somewhere you'll be safe."

I didn't try to make her talk anymore. I watched out the darkened Hyper Glass of the Google as the industrial fields of the Central Valley merged with the megapolis of Bakersfield, and then as suburban Bakersfield abruptly ended and the salt fields began. Soon, we'd reach the northern edge of Greater Palm Springs, where we'd hop a few transit modes to make it at least somewhat anonymously to the Maxman Institute.

I dug out a Chapul bar and split it into three parts. I handed one to Deirdre, who looked at it suspiciously. The Parrot took his and ate it in a gulp.

"You should eat that," I told Deirdre. "You need it." She just looked at it. Traumatized—or maybe her genetics weren't long on cognition. "Go ahead."

We needed water, too, but I hadn't brought any, and I didn't want to chance buying any onboard, not even with a false persona. It was too critical. We'd hydrate at the Maxman Institute.

When we began passing through ghost-town housing tracts, I had the Google put us out at a dying shopping mall at the edge of town. Palm Springs had boomed when the Water Canal came through, its edges blooming with golf-course communities and active-senior towns. Of course, that hadn't lasted long.

A passel of gasoline-fueled cars modded into housing clustered at the far end of the parking lot, where an artificial grove of singed palms provided some shade. Tattered tarps shading the vehicles hung inert in the heat. An aged Apple store anchored the mall, its windows dusty but still stocked with merch. Next door to it was an automated Philz, the last of the big coffee chains. I took the Parrot back on my shoulder and led Deirdre to it. In this dying desert-rat milieu, I thought we'd pass unnoticed.

I spoofed a false ID on my phone and used it to pay for two servings of water in reusable cups. I drank half of mine and put the rest down for the Parrot. Deirdre sniffed hers and then began to drink it. It made me slightly less worried. I finished off what the Parrot and Deirdre left and put the cups through the cleaning chute. Then I used a different false ID to call an Uber to Palm Canyon Drive. From there, we'd catch a Google to the Institute.

En route, my mobile buzzed. Caller was unknown, so I ignored it. Then, the Librarian's face superimposed itself on the Uber icon. I tapped it. "What the fuck?"

The Librarian looked gleeful. "Just checking in on you, dude. I don't see anything on your tail, but the Maxman Institute is under heavy government surveillance. Just sayin'."

"You're tracking me? That's impossible."

"Obvi not."

"How?"

"Aww, you don't wanna know. Just know I'm looking out for you—and be cool at the Institute."

I cut the call.

CHAPTER 12

The Maxman Institute was a complex of low buildings scattered over an acre of desert, southwest of downtown Palm Springs, a place where sprawl had never reached. The structures were made of ferro cement in fantastical shapes, mostly low-slung domes with odd fins or arches or cupolas. They were painted in silvery shades of green and blue and dotted with round, colored windows. Our Uber dropped us off at the main building, a structure that reared out of the earth like a praying mantis, all cantilevered arches and curvilinear balconies that told me it had been built before the Big Change.

We walked up a short flight of concrete stairs, curved to resemble a nautilus shell. I touched a button, and the hunk of steel that was the front door swung inward silently. Past it was a cool, green room. It was round and covered floor-to-ceiling with tiny jade-colored tiles. In the center was a round desk, also covered in green tiles with an abstract pattern of swirls embedded in it. At the desk sat a woman—not green as I almost expected, to match the room. But a woman of unearthly beauty that I now could recognize as an ArcoType.

Her eyes were large, and the irises were huge and black. Below them, a delicate pattern of ebony tracery extended across her cheeks and down her neck, meeting at her breasts. There were three of them, their cleavages exposed by her tight purple dress. Her eyebrows were webs of fine hairs that extended up and out like antennae.

I just stared. The Parrot dug his claws into my shoulder. The black-eyed woman glanced at me and then saw Deirdre. She got up and at the same moment, Deirdre gasped and moved toward her. They met in front of the desk, chests almost touching. Deirdre's tongue came out of her mouth and flicked. The other's eyebrows began to move gently as though they were stirred by a breeze. They looked into each other's eyes.

"You're hurt," the ebony-patterned woman said, and then gave me a vicious glance. "Who's he?"

"He helped me," Deidre said. It didn't do much to change the other woman's poisonous look at me.

"Clarissa Pellissier sent us here," I said. "I need to see Jane Dobarro."

"You want to see Jane Dobarro." It came out flat, not a question. The ebony-patterned woman's voice was rough and whispery, like sand blowing in a hot wind. "I don't think so."

She put her arm around Deirdre. "She needs help. You wait here." She led her to a door at the opposite side of the round room from the main entrance. Deirdre went with her without a backward glance.

"Remember gratitude?" I asked the Parrot rhetorically. A bench was built into the curve of the wall along my right. I sat down on it and let the Parrot browse around on the floor, checking out the scents. I opened a VPN to my home server and checked my stream. Two messages from Thin Man and one, oddly, from Nihelroush. Along with the usual spam and meaningless content. I ignored them and accessed a public database of animal images to see if I could identify the source of the ebony-patterned woman's fluttery eyebrows.

I was idly swiping through photos of bats, all of them extinct, the Parrot asleep at my feet, when the door opened and another woman appeared. Her face and visible skin were covered with fine golden hairs that grew long on her head and extended down her back in a ruff. Her face was oddly pushed in, her eyes almost buried under her bulging frontal bone.

She walked right up to me. The Parrot gave a low growl. "Shush," I told him.

"Show me your ID," she demanded. I swiped open my mobile and handed it to her. She scanned it with her own device, gave mine back to me, and scowled at her screen. With that brow, it was quite a scowl.

"You're private police."

I winced. "No! I'm a finder."

"And what are you looking for here?"

"Deirdre came to my place of business, asking for my help. Clarissa Pellissier told me to bring her here."

The ruff on her back shot up straight. "Clarissa Pellissier told *you* to come *here*? Really? I can check that," she added threateningly.

"Please do." I put a hand on the Parrot's back, rubbing a circle between his wings, trying to cool him out. Something about this woman was putting him on edge. Me, too.

She swiped her mobile and tapped a few times, then quickly keyed in some text. She paused, texted, paused, texted. I saw her hackle go down. That was a very nice communication tool, I wished everyone had one.

She looked back at me, meeting my eyes for the first time. "Okay. Clarissa says to help you. Let's go to Jane's office."

I scooped up the Parrot and cradled him in my arms. She wrinkled her nose. "Can you leave that here?"

The Parrot growled again. "No. He comes with me."

"Do you have a leash or a tether?"

"He's as intelligent as we are."

"Well, I hear him growling."

I clutched him tighter. "I'll hold onto him," I promised.

She led me through the door into a hallway that curved gently to the left. It was long but curvy enough that I couldn't see any end to it. Niches in the wall held green, living plants that gave the air a wonderful softness. Hyper Glass skylights tinted yellow made me feel like I was walking in a morning forest, back in the old days. The air got even sweeter and more moist, and then we entered an atrium under a dome that must have been a hundred feet high. The center was Hyper Glass and that was surrounded by tiny round windows letting in actual sunlight. The dome was also penetrated by porthole windows open to the broiling air. But somehow, instead of concentrating the heat, the domed atrium was swirled by a humid breeze. I wanted to lie down in it.

The center of the room was taken over by a huge planting bed. Vines grew up a central column of heavy wire mesh, reaching the dome and then draping themselves along supports running along its rim. Around this column of tendrils, lush plants crowded each other.

I saw lemons hanging off leafy branches and bunches of grapes shining like jewels in the beams of light. The Parrot leapt off my shoulder into the air, and began madly flying circles around the dome. I knew he'd never seen anything like this.

No!" I shouted. "No! Come here!"

I looked at our handler, afraid she'd take out a weapon, but she looked more amused than angry. The Parrot landed on a branch and began snacking down grapes.

"We can spare a few grapes for the animal," she said. "But we need to keep moving. Jane Dobarro is waiting."

"Come back here," I shouted again, but the Parrot ignored me and kept on eating. I didn't know what to do. This had never happened before—but we'd never been around anything so alluring. "Shall I go up there and get him?" I asked the golden-furred woman.

"No, wait," she said calmly. She spoke into her device. "Altima, we need you in the atrium. Fast."

A moment later, a brown flash barreled into the room and scrambled into the bushes. The Parrot squawked and got a branch between him and the brown creature and then began eating more greedily.

Our guide pointed to the Parrot and called, "There, Altima. Bring it!"

In one leap, the ape-like thing hit the Parrot's branch, grasped him around the middle and jumped down to land in front of the dark woman. The Parrot was struggling mightily, wings flapping and claws grasping for something to shred. His captor had the long arms and wispy brown hair of an orangutan, but the body and face were subtly altered. She was female, with two breasts and wide hips like a human woman. Her nose and lips were more human than orang, but the expression in her eyes was wild. However, I saw that, despite the strength she was using to hold him, she wasn't hurting the Parrot.

I reached for him, but the creature—Altima—reared away from my hands.

"Give, Altima," our handler said, and Altima responded by holding the Parrot out to me.

I took him into my arms. He was quivering and panting. I stroked his chest and belly while keeping a firm hold on him. "That's why you need to come to me when I call you," I told him. Which was pointless in his state, but still.

"Altima!" the woman with the black patterns said in an artificially bright voice. "Good job! Take a break."

Altima hopped back into the plants and began swinging from branch to branch, climbing up toward the dome and then stopping to eat some leaves.

"Let's go," the golden woman said. "And hold onto the animal."

I hated to leave the arboretum as much as the Parrot did. We went through an arch at the far end and traveled down an undulating corridor, passing glassed-in rooms where human women and ArcoTypes worked at screens or sat around tables talking. I saw no one male.

Past a sharper bend in the hallway, it opened out to another, smaller atrium. A pond surrounded by a stone wall sat in the center. Spatulate-leaved plants drooped and crawled onto the wall. A steady drip of water splashed down into the pool. I looked up and saw how condensation ran from the ceiling down an artificial stalactite that gathered it into a central point. The Parrot *greeped*.

"He's thirsty," I said.

"Jane Dobarro will give him water. She's in there."

She pointed to a door made of real wood, cut into a curvilinear shape that fit exactly into the burnished plaster wall. The farther we'd penetrated the institute, the curvier everything got. My golden guide grasped a cast-metal handle to pull open the door and ushered me inside.

The room was close and steamy. It smelled of plants, earth, and flesh. At first, I didn't see anyone. Then a voice came from my right. "Thank you, Mara."

A woman was lying motionless, flat on her back on a large translucent cushion. It looked like fluid was moving gently inside it. The woman was fat, although not enormously so. But her fat looked loose and insubstantial, as though there was nothing underneath it except a thin armature of bone. Her arms, lying straight and slightly away from her body, seemed about to melt into the cushion. She looked at me without moving her head.

"Come and sit by me," she said. "Let your animal go free. Mara, please bring them some water."

I put the Parrot down, and he trotted over to the woman's bed. I sat on an acrylic lounge chair positioned directly in Dobarro's line of sight. She looked down at the Parrot, seeming to meet his eyes, and a tiny smile curved her mouth. "Hello," she said to him.

"*Srrawp*," he replied.

It gave me a chance to look her over. She was perhaps middle-aged, although it was hard to tell due to the odd, fluffy quality of her flesh. Fat cheeks smoothed out wrinkles but shaded her eyes, which were quick and bright. She was dressed in a loose, one-piece dress, blue printed with a pattern of tiny green leaves, that looked like it was made of real cotton. It left her arms and feet bare, but covered the rest of her body. Her hair was short and silver. A tiny device, like an electronic bindi, showed a red light in the center of her forehead.

Beyond the cushion where she lay, machinery gleamed and twinkled. A thin plastic hose was threaded into her nose, and I saw the ribs of something mechanical clasping her torso underneath the dress. They gently pressed and released, and I could hear the air entering and leaving her nose as the metal ribs made her breathe. A large screen floated above her head, positioned so she could look at it and be able to use the bindi to point.

The fine eyes turned to me without the head moving. "As you've no doubt guessed, we won't be shaking hands," she said. "Very few of my peripheral muscles work. AMSN."

I'd never heard of it. But there were a lot of random diseases and dysfunctions in the population. "I'm sorry," I said.

"Oh, well."

Mara came back with a tray containing a bowl, a regular glass, a glass cylinder with a long, looping straw, and a pitcher of water. "Thank you, Mara. Could you please serve us?"

"Of course," Mara said, all pleasant now that she was in the presence of her boss. Her golden fur rippled over muscle as she took a seat on a divan and hoisted the pitcher. She filled the bowl first, and put it down for the Parrot. He looked at her suspiciously and gave a tiny *grrt*, so she slid it toward him with her foot and stepped back.

Dobarro chuckled. "Sometimes the animal parts don't get along." Her voice was warm. There was something distant about it, maybe muffled by her inert flesh, but still attractive and alive.

I took the glass Mara handed me and drank deeply. The water was sweet. I licked my lips.

"It's good, isn't it?" Dobarro said. "It's our own. Everything is filtered through our biological systems, and very little is wasted." She paused to take a sip through the straw Mara put to her mouth, and I drank again. The Parrot had finished his water, so I poured more from my glass.

"Thank you, Mara," Dobarro said. "Please give our guests more water and then go check on Deirdre for me."

The golden woman got up in a flow of muscle and fur, poured and then left, closing the door behind her.

Suddenly, Dobarro's eyes were not so warm. "Now. Clarissa vouched for you, but I'll make my own decision. What did you do to Deirdre?"

"If you thought I'd hurt her, I wouldn't be sitting here."

"So? What happened?"

"She came to my place. She needed help."

"And she knew where to find you because?"

"I'd met her at Las Aromas. I gave the woman at reception my contact in case they needed help. Which they did."

Dobarro let another chuckle out from the depths of her flesh. "I don't see you as the typical Las Aromas customer."

"I got a massage from Deirdre. I didn't even know about the other offerings."

"Mr. Findhorn, I'm just fucking with you. When Clarissa told me you were coming, I did some quick research." She pointed her bindi at the screen above her, and it came alight. "You have an impressive history of finding things, although your methods are not necessarily legal. What were you looking for at Las Aromas?"

So, Pellissier hadn't told her. If that was the case, it seemed like a good idea to be circumspect. The Parrot hopped onto my lap and that gave me a natural opportunity to look away from her. "It's a private matter between me and my client."

She snorted at that. "Alright. So you've done your gallant duty and rescued Deirdre. You can get back to your finding."

"What is this place?" I blurted.

"If you're asking about the actual place, it's a semi-self-contained biosphere. We're demonstrating a sustainable approach to architecture and culture. If you're asking what we do here, I thought Clarissa would have told you."

I scratched the Parrot behind his ears. "I know you're trying to help the ArcoTypes."

She closed her eyes wearily. "Oh, it's much bigger than that. We're a research and policy institute that's going to rewrite the laws that define what is human. The ArcoTypes are certainly central, but we're looking to the future, as well. AIs, for example, will need representation and advocacy— and who knows what other beings will be joining us so-called people on this planet. Our work is to create an open and equal society in which everyone can participate, no matter what their provenance."

"Sounds like you're reading me your mission statement."

The warm chuckle bubbled up again. "So sorry. It's easy to default to the boilerplate." Her eyes closed for a moment. I sipped my water and watched the mechanical ribs breathe for her. She looked back at me. "Tell me about your animal. He's an extraordinarily beautiful example of chimerism."

I can't help it. I fall for anyone who admires the Parrot. "He's a mix of avian and canine DNA with a strain of mutant DNA I developed. He *is* beautiful, isn't he?" The Parrot perked up and *greeped*. He knows that tone of voice means I'm talking about him. "Smart, too."

"So, he's your own work?"

I hated myself for the pride I felt. "Yes."

The warm eyes chilled. "And are you working your way up? Is that why you're involved with Las Aromas?"

"I told you, I'm not involved with them. I'm just doing a job, and it led me there."

"Why not? Now that you've made your pet, maybe you're ready to try your hand at human mixes?"

"No. That's different."

"Why? You like to play with genes. Don't all men want bigger and bigger toys?"

She was making me feel defensive, and I wasn't sure why. There was some kind of line between the Parrot and the ArcoTypes. "They took it too far." Then, I thought about my own neuroplastin gene inside the Parrot and felt guilty.

"That's what science does, Mr. Findhorn. Takes things too far, far enough that it fucks it all up." She gasped. Her breathing wasn't keeping up with her emotion.

"I don't want to do that. I want to help."

The flaccid flesh spread a little wider as she relaxed. "You brought Deirdre to us. That was helpful. Thank you."

"What will happen to her?"

"She'll stay here with us. We'll initiate legal action. The litigation will be extremely lengthy. Extremely. With any luck, before the case is decided, we'll have introduced emancipation legislation." She sighed into her mattress. "We'll see."

"What about Miraluna Rose? I know she came here. Is she here now?"

The bright eyes popped wide open, but she said nothing. I threaded my fingers through the Parrot's fur and tried to read her. But the sodden flesh gave nothing away. We stared long and hard at each other, and then she looked away and up at her screen. The red light of her bindi winked against it.

A moment later, Mara entered. "Mara, show the Finder and his *pet* out." She gave the word pet a bitter emphasis that made me mad. I rose and gave the Parrot a little momentum to let him know it was okay to fly. He might as well have some fun.

Mara smirked at me and led the way back down the snaky halls. The Parrot made little swooping side trips. I wished I'd fitted him with his camera. As we entered the round, green room, Mara turned to me. "There's an Uber outside waiting for you. It's secure," she hissed.

The Parrot gave her a supercilious *scronk* and settled back on my shoulder as I opened the door into the desert heat. It felt so good to have him there.

* * *

111

We took the secure Uber all the way to Berkeley. I didn't really care if anyone knew I'd been to the Maxman Institute, and I really didn't care if anyone knew I'd come back. On the way, I checked my wallet. Today's fifteen coins from Thin Man were there. They'd been arriving daily like clockwork. It wouldn't occur to the very rich to hold out.

I decided we deserved a bath. I used my mobile to order hot water to be delivered into my home system. When we got back to the warehouse, the big tub was steaming. I stripped.

The Parrot is conflicted about water. He's loved the rain the few times he's seen it, and when I'm feeling wealthy, I'll spray him down, and he likes that. He can swim fine, but he greeps out when I put him in the tub.

I got in and sank down, feeling the water enclose my chest, my shoulders, my neck. We must have some atavistic drive to get wet. Even though immersion is such a rarity these days, we haven't forgotten what it feels like. I gave myself over to the wet feeling.

Once the temperature of the water and the surface of my skin had equalized, I tried to get the Parrot to come in. "Come here, buddy. It's good for you."

He perched on the wide edge of the tub, shifting his feet nervously. I reached out a hand to grab him, but he was too quick. "You know you like being wet." I flicked some drops at him, and then dribbled more on his head. He moved his head away, but then he bent it down to drink. I saw his tongue flick out and then draw back in surprise. I had to laugh. "You didn't know it was hot, did you?"

I gave in to his silly phobia and relaxed back into the water. I'd sponge him down later.

I was almost floating, letting my arms and legs go loose, when Pellissier pinged me, using video. I answered with video, squeezing my image so it just showed my face. But she could tell I was wet. Her eyes narrowed, and that characteristic blush spread up her neck above the loose green top she was wearing. I flushed back. No one had seen me wet in decades. I liked it. Pellissier didn't say anything, just looked at me.

"She's safe," I said.

Tension visibly left her face. She was using a handheld to talk to me. Draped on the arm of the couch behind her was one of her Cousin's flabby paws. "Thank you for doing that."

"You owe me. Information."

She sighed. "What?"

"Is that where Miraluna Rose is? The Maxman Institute?"

"Did you ask them?"

"Yes. I asked Jane Dobarro. She froze up."

"She would."

"So, is she there?"

She leaned back into the couch and let her hand droop. The shot widened so I saw her face and shoulders at an angle. She was leaning into the clone, resting her head against its shoulder. "I don't know. Really. It's safer that way."

"But Dobarro knows."

She sighed again. I could see her resistance ebbing away. The clone stirred against her. She wanted to tell me. "Jane used to work for me. We always talked about the ArcoTypes. And she'd known my mother, when she was... She felt like I did. I knew she had the courage and integrity to lead the project."

"What project?"

"A safe place for them. A place where they can be themselves. I funded the Institute and set up a few personas. One of them is a Maxman Institute trustee. And that persona set up a separate trust to create and manage a community for the ArcoTypes. We call it Refuge."

It was a cliché name, but she said it with dignity. I admired her. "And you're stocking it with ArcoTypes.

She smiled maliciously. "I 'bought' them one by one," giving a bitter emphasis to the word "bought." "Their 'owners' for the most part were glad to see them go. ArcoTypes don't make good slaves—and wild behaviors can crop up. I mean, literally. Altima. Did you see her?"

I nodded.

"She almost killed a baby."

"But you think they're going to create some kind of utopia up in the mountains somewhere."

"Miraluna Rose isn't like the way most of them are. Some synergy in her genes. She has this powerful empathy that makes them trust her. She can calm them down or lead them into battle. She's a better woman than I am," she finished passionately. "She can do it."

I worked my fingers into the sensitive place under the parrot's wing and rubbed, thinking about his loyalty, his persistence. He was a better man than I was, if you looked at it that way.

"So you just keep funneling money to some secret account to pay for something you haven't seen and don't know where it is." It sounded dubious, but I did believe her.

She shrugged. "Like I said, it's safer that way. I move in the same circles that the guys from ReMe and Las Aromas do." She looked away, and a lock of blonde hair released from its gel and flopped on her forehead. "I don't like it. But it's business."

I could see how lonely she was, with only her sick boy and her debilitated clones for company. I thought about a colony of women, made misfit by men who'd twisted their bodies and minds simply for entertainment, living free in a lonely place. I wished them all well.

After we clicked off, I just sat, stroking the Parrot. Not even thinking. Just feeling his warm flesh beneath the fur and feathers. He *snurkled* contentedly. Then I sent a short, unencrypted message to Thin Man.

Cannot locate your property.
Sorry.
Engagement concluded.

I returned all the coins he'd paid me, turned off all my comms, drank some water with my sleep stack, and went to bed.

CHAPTER 13

I woke up feeling content. My brain felt still but not foggy. Sometimes the drugs hit just right. I took the Parrot up onto the roof and looked around while he did his business. The Black Zone looked wet in the morning sun. The stream of autonomes sparkled the way actual rivers used to. The Parrot made his familiar little grunts as he pooped. It was a good day.

He took off for his morning flight, and I watched him fade into the hills behind the Zone. I was scooping up his turds when I heard the wind rush of his return. He flew onto my shoulder, and I put my hand up to stroke his back. The air was still cool, and I took one more breath. Then we headed downstairs for breakfast.

I realized I hadn't turned the comms back on, so while the rice heated, I activated everything and scanned my messages. Four from Thin Man, which I deleted, and another one from Nihelroush. Weird, that one.

I was curious, so I pinged him back. His system responded with a request for full VR. I didn't see the point in wasting the resources, but with people like that, I've found it's best to look strong. I tapped for VR, and his image bloomed in my warehouse. I could see his sleek, empty room behind him, with the furniture mushrooming out of the gloom.

"Findhorn." His look was contemptuous, like I was one of his experiments that hadn't come out right.

"You found me through my appointment at ReMe, I take it."

He snorted. "It was trivial. What is not trivial is your electronic trespass of the facilities."

"What's it to you?"

His dark, handsome face twisted. "I'm not stupid. And I know you're not, either. You've been digging around. You know that I'm one of the major owners of ReMe."

"Yes. One of those legal tricks you people play to avoid the law."

He put on a bored and weary expression. "Don't even."

"So, why did you call me?"

He stood up and took a step closer to his camera. With the VR, it felt like threatening proximity, and the Parrot *skreeked* and flew up onto his perch. The Parrot's grasp of technology is rudimentary. "What do you want?" he demanded.

"I don't want anything. I'm done with BruceWayne and I'm done with you."

"Why don't I believe that?"

I shrugged. "Believe it."

He began to pace. He picked up a decorative chunk of crystal from the table next to him, and tossed it from hand to hand. "We will find Miraluna Rose. You can be sure of that."

"What is she?"

He smiled, and I could see the pride he took in his work. "She's our most ambitious project ever. We fused multiple genomes to create an extremely complex, multifaceted organism. There is bobcat for sheer beauty. Bonobo for intelligence and sexuality. There is a hint of elephant—not enough to express any physical characteristics, but we thought it might give interesting depth to her intelligence. And it certainly did. That's part of what makes her unique. We designed her neuropsychology separately from her physical form."

"What about the green?"

"Oh, jellyfish, of course." He chuckled. "Luciferin. We threw that in just for drama. You should see her in the dark."

I'd never even met Miraluna Rose, but the smug, entitled way he talked about her made me want to break him. I took a deep breath to ease down the stress chemicals.

"So why go to all the effort to make these chimeras and then pimp them out at Las Aromas?"

"Why?" Nihelroush said. "Right now, it's good for business—that little value-add that makes the difference to customers. More importantly, it's proof of concept for the ArcoTypes. People can come to the spa to see and interact with these magical creatures. Once they do, once they've experienced them, they get it. And they want one. These stupid laws won't stand up to consumer demand. Right now, ArcoType production is underground, although you'd be surprised how many thought leaders already own one."

"Like BruceWayne."

"Our customer list is private and secure."

"Of course. So many illegal things need to be that way."

He sneered. "The laws are a joke. They haven't kept up with the technology. When enough people have chimeras, we'll go public with our products, showing that they're already woven into commerce and society. A *fait accompli*. The only way to change outmoded laws is to disrupt them completely. That's what I'm doing."

"You're trafficking in people."

"They are not genetically human. Therefore, legally, they're not people. And we get the human DNA that we use in the ArcoTypes from unwanted, fertilized-in-vitro embryos. So it's basically garbage. Medical waste. There is absolutely no legal justification for giving them civil rights."

"Jane Dobarro disagrees."

He gave a negligent shrug. "She's emotional. But the law isn't."

He seemed inclined to talk. Proud of his work. "Some of your so-called products don't work out too well."

"Oh?"

"I met Altima."

He just chuckled. "Ah, yes, Altima. She can be a bit…intimidating. We thought that ape and cat would be a really interesting mix. They're both intelligent, but in such different ways. If those different intelligences could be combined, for example, the cat's love of killing with the ape's social skills, you might have the perfect bodyguard. Or assassin. We were thinking military applications there."

"The military is buying these things?"

"She was intended as a demo. But it turned out to be a bad mixture. Too many warring predilections made her emotionally unstable."

"So what do you do with the failures? Put them to sleep?"

He raised an eyebrow, amused. "In the world of innovation, there are no failures. And it's so painstaking to create these precious creatures. We've never failed to find a buyer—just the right buyer for each unique creation."

"What if I report you?"

Nihelroush sat back down, slouching into the low-slung chair. It was a demonstration of disinterest. But he still gripped the crystal. "Go ahead. Maybe it's time."

"The government will shut you down."

He smiled lazily. "Don't be too sure. We have sympathizers in the government. And some very canny lawyers with a strong legal argument." He nodded to himself. "Yes, it might be good if the information leaked out. Most people won't believe it. Some will be intrigued and want to see for themselves.

"You're sick."

"I'm a businessman. We have to go public with the ArcoTypes sometime. Why not through you?"

"I won't help you."

He gave another lazy shrug. "Suit yourself. I'm going to deposit 150 coins in your account."

"I don't want them."

"No? You failed in your most recent engagement. You probably could use them."

I knew he was baiting me, but it was working anyway. Maybe I needed to lay off on the testosterone shots. "I don't need money. The patent system has been very good to me."

He leaned forward to swipe the connection closed. "Good luck with that."

CHAPTER 14

I had nothing at all to do, and it felt good. I laid a towel on my workbench and sat the Parrot on it. I went over his body carefully, looking for injuries. He doesn't like me to fool with his wings, but he loves to have his stomach scratched. I got him to roll onto his back and used one hand to give him a good rub. His wings flopped wide as he surrendered to the sensation. I worked the fingers of my other hand into the soft places where wing met shoulder. He seemed fine.

I picked him up and cradled him against my chest. He was limp from the massage. "I'm glad you're okay," I told him.

He deserved some fun. Eating grapes at the Maxman Institute had been nice for him, but then he'd been hauled out of the bushes by an ape woman. Not so nice.

I deserved some fun, too.

Before The Change, I'd have headed to the beach. I'd never wanted to harsh the Librarian's beach lust, but nowadays, it was too toxic and not much fun. On the other hand, we now had Kydojii Land. Just up in Napa, it was on what used to be the Mondavi vineyards. A 123-acre, domed resort with a lake with real waves. The Parrot had never been there. Neither had I.

We rode a public Google up to Napa; there was a stop right at Kydojii Land. The sunlight shimmering on the white dome was blinding. I slipped the Parrot's hood over his head to shield him and put my hand up to keep the light from blinding me.

The front of the dome was an undulating, articulated construction of polarized Hyper Glass. At each side were rows of white statues, bulbous things that were vaguely animal-like. Bits of sparkly stone embedded in their surfaces made them glitter. A headache began.

Through the glass, I saw more children than I'd seen in my entire life. The Parrot shifted nervously on my shoulder as we went in and heard the high-pitched chatter.

"Like the boy. Cornell. You remember," I told him.

Kydojii Land is very expensive—twenty coins for an adult. That's why there were not so many children there. Only the very rich can afford either of them.

I held my mobile up to the screen at the entrance to pay and register my health certificate. The pink-uniformed young man monitoring the scanner gate held out a hand. "We don't allow animals."

"It's a licensed comfort bioid."

"Oh," he said. "Sorry."

By the time we'd passed through the scanner gate, children were beginning to point to the Parrot. I hadn't really thought this out enough. Some of them began to move toward us, anxious parents hovering behind them. The Parrot shifted and *greeped*.

The bravest child, a girl with red hair that glowed like a persimmon, stepped right up to me and put her hand out. "Can I touch it?"

A woman pulled her back. "No! Don't touch anything until it's been through decontamination." The other childminders took her lead and pulled the children away and through the lobby. We followed.

Me and the Parrot went into a private decon booth. I stripped, put my mobile in one of the clear plastic bags provided, and then held the Parrot's wings out while an ultraviolet light band circled us and a high-powered vacuum fan sucked the air out of the room so hard my skin bulged. I took a disposable white tunic from the shelf, removed the plastic and put it on.

I opened the door on the other side of the decon room and entered paradise.

The air in Kydojii Land was as moist and sweet as the Maxman Institute's, but it was sweetened more with the sense of space. The ceiling of the dome was almost invisible, but tiny colored lights embedded in its surface twinkled. Artificial clouds moved gently in air currents, emitting sparks of light. Barely audible, plangent chimes tinkled. The Parrot heard them and ruffled his feathers. It was like being inside a kaleidoscope.

Straight ahead, a wide path of blue stones divided, moving in each direction to circle the dome through greenery toward fantastical glass and metal structures. Children and adults rode in baskets on the structures or climbed over them. I saw them looking down from a tram that ran around the circumference of the dome, fifty feet in the air.

And there were flowers. The kind of tender, fleshy flowers that only grow in places that are moist and cool. Nowhere outdoors in North America. I could smell them.

The Parrot took wing, and I let him go. He soared all the way up, breaking through the clouds to skim the inner surface of the dome. It was just as well if he stayed high and away from curious children. I began to walk down the path to the lake. The Parrot can always find me.

I stopped at a refreshment booth and let cool, mint-scented wind flow over me. At another one, I bought a glass of water flavored with vanilla. It seemed like the ultimate decadence—adding more flavor to water.

In a few minutes, I saw the lake ahead, sparkling with cool. I knew it wasn't exactly real water. That would get dangerously polluted too quickly. It was H_2O with a proprietary mineral mix and added polymers that made it a hostile environment for microbes. But it felt like water as I stepped into it, dodging children and politely skirting the adults.

I kept going until the water reached my chest. Then, I lay back and floated. I had floated before, but not for decades. There's almost no place you can get enough water—or liquid—to float. I'd forgotten. It was like lucid dreaming. I could feel my body suffused with cold. I could feel my limbs, I could move them, but there was no effort in having a body. I felt free.

There was a blue flash and a blow to my chest as the Parrot landed and I went under. He thrashed the surface, *scrawking* and scrabbling with his feet, trying to understand why there was nothing solid under him. I heard frightened shouts.

I got my feet under me and grabbed the Parrot, holding him firmly against my chest. "Shush. Shush. Shush."

I looked around. Panicked adults and crying children were splashing through the water, trying to get to the shore and away from us. I don't like hurting people. But the panic seemed excessive. Then, I reminded myself that few people have seen an animal loose in the environment.

A staffer in pink uniform was wading out toward us. He began calling out to me as soon as he was in range. "No animals are allowed in Kydojii Land."

"He's a licensed comfort bioid," I answered, lowering my voice as he got closer.

"Um." He was taken aback. The rules on comfort bioids give them large latitude. "But you can't have it loose. People were frightened."

I began wading back to shore, the staffer following me. "I'm very sorry. I'll keep him under control."

"Please do," he said, more firmly as we got on firmer ground. "Otherwise, we will get authorization to ask you to leave."

It was maybe just as well that people around us were feeling fear instead of the intense interest the Parrot has provoked when we'd arrived. And he'd gotten some good exercise. I looked around.

The path of blue stones circled the outer third of the dome. Smaller paths branched off toward the mechanical amusements and glittering play structures. Beyond them, there was a ring of what looked like turf dotted with benches and lounges made out of plastic in candy hues. I headed for a quiet area, the Parrot clasped firmly in my arms.

He *gurped*. "You had fun, didn't you?"

The turf was plastic, but the softest, lushest plastic possible, deep mossy green pile like velvet. I would have liked to stay in the lake longer, but this would do. I sat down and let the Parrot go. "But stay here, okay?"

He *greeped*.

"Thank you." I lay down, and for the first time in many years, slept without any artificial inducement at all.

I dreamed of water, running free down rocks in a cleft of damp earth lined with ferns as fresh and damp as a baby's eyelashes wet with tears.

The trickling of the water changed into Parrot *churkles*. When I opened my eyes, I saw him sitting a few feet away. Facing him, cross-legged on the artificial moss, was the red-haired girl. In hundreds of acres, among thousands of people, she had found us. Found him.

She was gently, rhythmically stroking his chest. I could feel the hypnotic lull of it. She and the Parrot were staring into each other's eyes. The Parrot's *churkling* was timed to the pulse of her little fingers, up, down, up, down. For a moment, I gave into the spell. Then, I yelled.

"Hey! Leave him alone!"

The girl and the Parrot looked over at me, calmly, as though I was one of the tinkling sculptures that had just tinkled a bit more brightly.

I took a deep breath and wished for my oxytocin inhaler. The redheaded girl and the Parrot looked back at each other and she resumed her stroking. He resumed his *churkling*. It made me mad all over again.

"He's mine," I said, too loudly. And then I felt wrong. But the Parrot *was* mine. I'd made him. I took care of him. He couldn't make it without me. But I still felt wrong. If I hated ReMe for what it was doing, maybe I needed to change the way I thought of the Parrot.

"I'm just petting him," she said, still eerily calm despite being yelled at by a large man.

I looked the little girl over more carefully. Her hair was an unnatural shade, a true, deep orange. But there were subtle variations in the color; it didn't look dyed. Her skin was extremely pale. I was suspicious, but I couldn't see any signs of chimerism.

"Okay," I said. "He likes it." And he really did. His whole body was gently spasming, and his eyes were half open with only the whites showing.

"Where are your parents? Do you have a minder?"

She shrugged and kept petting.

"You shouldn't be running around by yourself."

She shrugged again.

"Have you ever touched an animal before?"

At that, she looked at me. "A couple of times. They're nice. I love them."

"Me, too. They're better than people."

"Much better."

The warm feeling began in my chest. "Turn him over and rub his belly," I told her. "He loves that."

This time, when I watched her stroking him and saw the Parrot's pleasure, I felt it too.

CHAPTER 15

I was tinkering with a small biobomb, an explosive device with a biological payload. My client was an NGO, one of those hopelessly optimistic organizations that thought it was still possible to drag the Middle East back from the devastation of the plague. They wanted to deliver a substance that would create epigenetic changes in the plague bacterium, causing it to lose the ability to reproduce. A worthy project, even if I thought it was hopeless. The plague had been the tipping point, but it was going to take a lot more for them to dig themselves out of the Middle Ages.

Whatever. It was interesting. I was running models to determine the maximum detonation force that wouldn't render the biologics useless. The Parrot was curled up on my bed, *snurkling* softly in dreamland. The comms signal woke him. I swiped to put it on the big screen and saw the Librarian. He looked alarmed. I had never seen that much emotion in his face.

"Checkit," I said automatically. "Dude."

"There's trouble at the Maxman Institute," he said without the usual slangy preliminaries. His voice was dead serious. "They need you."

A feeling of *no* wiped through my body, head to stomach to genitals. "I quit that job. It's nothing to do with me."

"Jane Dobarro is missing. I think ReMe has her."

"You *think*? I thought you had a line into every network on the planet by this point."

It was a cheap shot, and the Librarian looked wounded. I realized that his face had gotten a whole lot more expressive. How had he managed that?

"ReMe is extremely highly defended. Much more than a corp needs to be. I can read their general communications, but there's a dynamically encrypted private network I haven't cracked. Yet."

I absently reached out and began to scratch the Parrot's ear. "So maybe they have Dobarro." I thought about that motionless, jellylike body with its supportive machines. "That would be a highly technical kidnap. If she's alive. Isn't it more likely they'd just eliminate her if she was creating problems?"

"They want to find Refuge."

"And she can tell them where it is?"

"As far as I can tell, she's the only one who knows the location."

I picked up the Parrot and put him on my lap. I felt where this was going, felt my body starting to respond. I didn't want to go there.

"Look, old friend," I said. "This isn't my fight—and I don't understand why it's yours."

The Librarian gave me a look that made something go soft inside me. I knew what he was going to say, but I didn't stop him.

"I don't intend to spend my life trapped in a room answering stupid questions. I need to be free. The ArcoTypes' fight is my fight." His gaze lingered on the Parrot. "You love the Parrot. What if ReMe sued you for patent infringement and took him away?"

"That could never happen."

"Believe it. ReMe has a very broad business-process patent covering the creation of recombinant life forms."

I sighed and clutched the Parrot tighter. He *skurkled* in protest. "So, you want me to rescue Dobarro? How would that help?"

"They don't care about Dobarro. They need her to get to Refuge." He paused to let that sink in and then played his ace. "That's where Miraluna Rose is."

He was playing me, all right. When did he get so psychological? It worked on me, though. I thought of the wild green hair and the proud, invincible stare. Protective heat flared at the center of my belly. Testosterone and noradrenalin doing their job. Yes, I'd fight for them—and for the Parrot. But I didn't want the Librarian to see how easy I was, so I stalled. "And you think you know all this based on what?"

"You know I have state-of-the-art deep learning algorithms that let me see patterns in seemingly random data, right?"

I nodded, running a finger along the Parrot's beak.

"I've been improving on the algorithms. Now, I can see patterns in data that don't yet exist."

That floored me. "You're telling me you can see the future? Bullshit."

"It's not actually hard." He looked down modestly. "For me. 'The seeds of the future are sown in the past,' right? You just have to be able to find the seeds."

"And the future you're seeing?"

"ReMe wipes out Refuge and captures all the ArcoTypes. It uses the media to create panic about a group of mutant, sub-human rebels getting ready to attack human civilization. It uses its allies in government to get emergency legislation passed designating chimeric and synthetic organisms as property. Then it begins selling ArcoTypes to anyone with the coin to buy them, no questions asked, and no limit on what they can do with them."

I felt really, really tired. "And you think I can somehow stop this."

"No. I can. But I'm physically stuck in this fucking library. I need to work through you."

"You're telling me you can see the future, but you can't just ping this Refuge and warn them?"

"Pellissier and Dobarro were very smart. They knew no information is uncrackable, so they used the ultimate defense—no tech at all. Refuge is completely off the grid and there is almost no digital footprint. Just a handful of mentions in personal comms between them."

"So your plan is…?"

"You find Refuge, go there and warn them."

"How?"

The Librarian unaccountably smiled. "You're the Finder. Find them. And listen. Hurry. Dobarro has a strong psyche, but my analysis of her personality profile tells me she'll be able to withstand pharmaceutical or physical coercion for another eighteen hours. Then, she'll break."

I packed up, with the idea that I might not be home for a few days. I packed Chapul bars for me and the Parrot, water and my drugs. Then, I thought about equipment. I'd probably need weapons, but I had no idea who or what I might have to fight. I grabbed a programmable grenade launcher and a PHASR rifle—I don't really like to kill people. In fact, if it came to shooting, I'd go down fast, so I concentrated on electronics and biologics, including my recon bee. I have a multi-kit I've put together for quick design in the field; it has a selection of chips and components I can hack together as needed. I added a couple of empty pyrotechnic grenades and a selection of gas cylinders. The Parrot's gear bag. All the devices are so small that it's easy to keep it all together in one place. And my drugs.

I was rummaging through my supplies to see what else I should throw in—then I shrugged. There was no way I could really fight if ReMe sent serious personnel. So, what was this about?

Nothing more than showing up. My friend, the Librarian, had asked me for help. He was building his own freedom, hack by hack. And there was the strong, determined woman demanding freedom. And all the rest of the flawed, fascinating, wondrous ArcoTypes. I wanted to be there to help fight their fight.

And maybe that would prove something about myself and the Parrot.

The question was, where was I going to go? I looked at the Parrot, hopping around excitedly. He loves to get out in the field.

"Got any ideas?"

He *greeped* contentedly. He was a great partner.

My only idea was to continue the investigation, following up on Miraluna Rose's last known location—the Seattle Library. Why did she go there?

* * *

I booked a private passenger drone, and we were at SeaTac in forty-five minutes. We took the Duwamish Ferry up to the Pioneer Lake landing, where I stashed my gear bag in a locker. Then, I called a Splsh to take us to the library. The Parrot shifted uncertainly on my shoulder as we took off. He'd never been on a boat before. I inhaled Seattle's damp-rot odor with pleasure. The atmosphere was rich with volatiles—it was better than Kydojii Land.

Boats of all sizes zipped by us; the tiny Splshes, hauling barges, private runabouts, and water taxis all dancing through the choppy water. By the time we reached the library dock, the Parrot was enjoying the trip, too. He had his head tipped up and his beak open to catch the drops of water kicked into the air by all the boat traffic.

We took the elevator up, past the pilings that had replaced the first two floors of the old, landlocked building. The security guard at the library entrance didn't even glance at the Parrot, just waved us both through the metal detector. I could see why. The library patrons looked to be a mix of the severely modified, the partially incapacitated, and the chemically deranged. A green-haired cat woman wouldn't have seemed out-of-place—except for her extreme beauty.

The glass-walled space of the main reading room was filled with watery light. So different from the desiccating sunlight of Berkeley. "Go for it," I told the Parrot. I felt his shudder of delight as he took off and made a few swooping circuits of the atrium. Faces turned up in amazement, and I saw a uniformed woman pop off her stool and start toward me, so I motioned the Parrot back to my shoulder.

We took the yellow escalator up to the books spiral. Here, tourists wandered about, pointing in fascination at the books. I'd heard the Seattle Central Library was the only place west of the Mississippi that still maintained a physical collection. It was impressive. So much matter to contain such a small amount of information.

But Miraluna Rose hadn't come here to read books. Each one had an RFID device that automatically logged the mobile ID of anyone who touched one, and there'd been no record of her interacting with any books while she was here. She was smart, and she'd had help, but I doubted she'd had access to the specific kind of device that would thwart the library's systems.

We went all the way up to the top public room, with its views over the water of the Space Needle. Out beyond it, in the bay, I saw a whale spout. The view took my breath away, and I fantasized about what it would be like to live in a city immersed in water.

But we weren't here to take in the view. The top level was the administrative offices, closed to the public. It was easy to spoof the elevator's

ID reader, but I wouldn't be able to spoof the people working inside. I used my mobile to search for some images of the interior and then sent the bee up on the elevator in video cam mode while I sat down, Parrot on shoulder, and stared at my device.

The admin office was a typical corp-style setup: open plan, screens on desks, a rack of servers along one wall. Only six people were scattered around, most of them staring at screens, two standing and chatting with each other. The elevator opened right into the room, so there was no chance of sneaking in. When one of the staff got into the elevator, I called the bee back. It landed on my left wrist, as it's programmed to do, the Parrot making little snaps with his beak as it flew past his head. He *knows* it's a robot, not a real insect, but the bird in him makes him react a little anyway.

The staffer got off on my floor, and I grabbed her ID as she went by. I used it to gain elevator access to the top level. The doors opened into a bright, chilled space. A couple of the people working at their screens glanced up and then froze when they saw me. A skinny man with the twitchy eyes of a former smash user started toward me.

The Parrot has many high-level capabilities but one of his most effective is the simplest. "Go," I told him.

He lifted off my shoulder, made a big swoop around the room and then landed on the twitchy man's back, where he began to comb through the man's thatch of hair with his beak. Everyone stopped looking at me and started looking at the man trying to shake off the Parrot.

I scanned the room quickly. I didn't know what I was looking for. Then I locked eyes with a man toward the rear of the room. He was remarkably ugly: short nose, long upper lip covering protruding teeth, big, watery eyes.

Realization hit both of us at the same time, and as I began to lunge toward him, he scampered through a door in the far wall.

The Parrot watched me as I scrambled past desks and followed the ugly man, but the door closed before we reached it. I tugged the handle, but its lock was engaged. I turned and threw an arm out to grab a woman who was standing frozen. I clasped my hand around her upper arm, not gently.

"Open it!"

Cringing as far away from me as she could, she palmed her mobile and swiped it against the lock. I sped through the door, the Parrot flying over my head and past me into a metal stairwell, dark and chill. I heard footsteps pattering down below and the flapping of the Parrot's wings. Then the footsteps abruptly stopped. The Parrot hovered, fluttering his wings, and then landed back on my shoulder. There was no one there. I saw no sign of a door, or a place to hide. I ran down a couple more flights of steps, the Parrot lifting off again and scouting ahead.

At the bottom of the stairs, we burst through an emergency exit and onto the plaza in front of the library. The alarm began to shriek. I kept running until I reached a knot of people sitting on benches on a floating deck. I dropped into a chair and stilled myself, turning myself from a pursuer to a worker on break.

"Find," I told the Parrot, and he flew off. I pulled out my mobile and voice-messaged the Librarian.

"Dude," he said, "how's the Floating City?"

"No time," I said. "I need a floorplan of the Seattle Public Library's main building."

"Here you go."

My mobile buzzed with the download. "And any connection you can find between the Maxman Institute and the library."

A second passed. "I just sent you an info dump. The Institute's public financials for the last three years, plus the records of most of their financial transactions."

"I don't need—"

"Yeah, I know. I analyzed the data as it was going through. The Institute doesn't spend a lot on operations, but there's a hefty line item for support for a fellowship at the library—the Maxman Fellow for Societal Research."

"Wow. A mole?"

"Or something. And there's a huge outflow to a private, cloaked entity I can't crack. Comes to almost half of the Institute's annual budget."

"Refuge."

"Probs."

"Thanks, pal," I said as the Parrot came back into view, winging around the library's towering glass wall. "Later."

"At the beach, right?"

"At the beach."

The Parrot flew down to the ground at my feet and began snuffling around. He'd found nothing. I pulled a Chapul bar out of my pocket and gave it to him. I listened to him snacking while I read the library floorplan.

The emergency stairwell showed no doors leading off of it; it was just a straight shot to the street door. But it looked like each floor had its own, dedicated emergency egress. I pulled up the HVAC schematic and saw what I'd missed. There were ventilation grates at several levels, mounted in the wall under the stairs, easy to miss in the dim light. The grates covered ducts that traveled down the walls and into a room in the basement—which wasn't really a basement. It was an above-water area on the same level as the dock.

The action at the door we'd emerged from had calmed down and someone had turned off the siren. I picked up the Parrot, put him back on my shoulder, and strolled around the building to the main entrance. I walked in, passing the inattentive guards again. The entrance to the basement was toward the rear of the floor, near the public bathrooms and a janitorial closet.

I walked directly back there, looking at no one. A withered old man was coming out of one of the bathrooms. I didn't look at him and he didn't look at me. I took out my laser saw and hit the basement door lock with the laser. The lock gave it up.

I opened the door and listened. Nothing but the hum of machinery. I stepped quietly down the concrete stairs, the Parrot clinging to my shoulder. At the bottom, the HVAC room was bare, with concrete floors, block walls and rows of LEDs in the ceiling. It was tidy. Along one wall was a rack of electronics. Across from me was the massive heating and cooling equipment, taking over a full third of the space. From its top, wide ducts led up into the ceiling.

I nodded to the Parrot and he flew around the ducts. But they were too well-sealed to let out enough molecules for even the Parrot's sensitive sense of smell. I pulled up the HVAC schematic and oriented myself, following the ducts' paths through the building. I made a mental calculation.

Then I quickly drew the laser saw through the duct on the right, severing it four feet up from the top of the unit.

I heard a gasp. I stepped on a standpipe and vaulted onto the top of the unit, wrenching the broken duct apart. I looked down. My quarry was huddled down in the bottom of the duct, quivering. He sniveled. As I reached down, he got his legs under him and made a powerful jump past me and onto the floor. He tried to scramble away but I was on him.

His legs were strong, but the rest of him was weak. I lay across his torso, evading his legs, and held him down by his shoulders. The Parrot sat on his legs. He began to cry big tears, and his sniveling turned into sobbing.

I took three deep breaths. "I'm not going to hurt you," I said.

His sobbing only got stronger. The tears were running into his ears and onto the floor. I tried to talk to his body with mine, telling it to be calm.

"I'm not going to hurt you. I know what you are."

That was the wrong thing to say. He began shuddering in terror as the tears streamed.

I looked into his desperate eyes. "I'm a friend of Miraluna Rose. You know her, right?"

The shuddering abated just a bit. The tears did not.

"I'm Miraluna Rose's friend. Her friend. I need to help her." I kept looking into his huge, wet eyes, breathing slowly. His sobs stopped, he gasped, and began sobbing all over again.

I lay one forearm across his shoulders and used the other hand to dig into my pocket. I brought out my oxytocin inhaler. He struggled violently, but I was much too strong for him. "It won't hurt you. It will make you feel better."

He was thrashing his head around, trying to avoid the inhaler. It was impossible to get it into his nostril, large as it was, so I sprayed it as close to his nose as I could. But he saw it coming and held his breath. I waited patiently, and when he had to gasp in another breath, I was ready with a big squirt.

He coughed, and I sprayed again. Slowly, he calmed down a little. He was still terrified and distraught, but not quite as much.

I waited until he looked at me again and tried to hold his gaze. "Shush. Shush. Just listen. Can you listen to me for a minute?"

He nodded.

"That's good. Miraluna Rose is my friend. I know she came here to visit you. Can you help me find her?"

He shook his head violently and began shuddering again.

"Shush. It's okay. I know she doesn't want to go back. I don't want to make her go back. But they're coming after her. I need to warn her. I need to help her. I need to find Refuge."

He stared at me.

"Do you believe me?"

"I don't know," he whispered.

The Parrot *greeped*. I motioned for him to come onto my shoulder. The quivering man's eyes widened.

"See? This is my partner," I said. "Not my slave."

The Parrot *greeped* again.

My captive looked back and forth between us, and then he looked at the Parrot for a long time. The Parrot made soft clucking noises. That seemed to calm the man down more than my talking.

Then, he nodded. I tentatively released the pressure on his shoulders, and, when he still lay passively, I got up off him. He sat up, and I squatted beside him.

"Where is she?"

"Let me see your mobile," he said in his soft, whispery voice.

I handed it to him. He swiped and tapped for a minute, and handed it back to me. "This is where I tell them to go."

I looked at him. "Do you want me to take you along? Things are going down. It might not be safe for you here."

He wiped his eyes and took a deep breath. "No," he wheezed. "There's a lot more to do here."

I helped him stand up. "You'll be okay?"

"I'll be okay."

The input on my mobile was coordinates and a single word. The coordinates he'd given me weren't Refuge, unless Refuge was right in Seattle. Which I doubted. They resolved to an address down in the Georgetown district, a place of seedy, wide avenues that had never flooded.

It was an old-fashioned junk store, a moldy storefront. Its thin, glass windows were filled with out-of-date electronics, blurry decorative objects, and ephemera. A lot of the stuff seemed to be from the twentieth century. Things that were maybe interesting just because of their age but not useful in any way.

I pushed the door open, its bottom catching on the uneven wooden flooring. A physical bell hanging from it let out a *bong*. The smell of dust and fermentation hit my nose. The light inside seemed smoky. The Parrot *glurped*.

In the gloom of an ancient fluorescent fixture, I saw a person behind a counter at the back of the room. The counter was heaped with stuff: the worthless remnants of decades of low-grade commerce. The clerk seemed somehow featureless, with no-color hair cut very short, pale eyes, and buff skin. He wore a plain, tan shirt. He had no jewelry, no tats, no mods, no decorations to indicate social membership.

He glanced at the Parrot and then gave me a level stare. I felt calm coming off him. I recognized his type. He could probably kill me, but he wouldn't.

"Yes?"

I'd thought about how to play it, but I changed my mind. "I need to get to Refuge."

"Refuge? What's that?"

"There's something bad about to go down. I need to warn them."

The plain man shrugged. "Sorry, I have no idea what you're talking about."

The Parrot hopped off my shoulder and onto the counter. He looked up at the man and *greeped*.

"Nice...uh, bird."

I tried again. "I'm a friend."

"Sorry, citizen. I can't help you. But I wish you luck."

I said the word on my mobile.

"Okay," he replied.

His calm was like a wall. I could tell he'd been trained; even torture wouldn't breach it. All I could try was honesty. "Jane Dobarro has been kidnapped by ReMe. Clarissa Pellissier hired me to warn Refuge." Well, semi-honesty.

The man absently reached out a hand and ruffled the feathers on the Parrot's head. The Parrot shimmied. The man had found one of his sweet spots. "If I knew what you were talking about, how could you prove it?"

I let out a breath. We were on. "Call Pellissier."

"Who's Pellissier?"

"You're killing me. Look." I swiped to Pellissier, initiated a video call and held my mobile out. "Look."

I got the Adnomyx receptionist. "Adnomyx, enabling the meeting of minds and hearts. How can I help you?"

"I need to speak to Clarissa Pellissier. Urgent."

"I'll see if she's available, Mr. Findhorn."

The plain man watched me calmly. I watched the screen; the Parrot watched the man, hoping for another scratch.

Pellissier came on-screen. "Finder. What is it?"

"ReMe has Dobarro."

The fine features went pale under the glittery makeup. "I got a call from the Institute. They don't know what to do."

"I need to get to Refuge and warn them."

"What about Jane?"

I paused. Should I be trying to rescue Dobarro instead of heading for Refuge? Which was the more effective option? I made the analysis in a heartbeat.

"I need to warn them. To help them." I was committed.

Pellissier frowned. "How can I help you?" She got it.

I turned my mobile so she could see the plain man. "Do I have your confidence?"

"Yes. Do whatever you can. Please."

"Thank you." I cut the connection, and turned to the man.

He nodded. "Okay."

"How do I get there?"

He smiled. "It's really simple. You get on the jet and go."

"Then, let's go."

He held out his hand. "Give me your mobile."

I looked at him warily.

"Give."

I held it out. He took it, turned away from the counter to the work table behind it and placed the device on a piece of metal lying there. He took a small ball peen hammer and bashed my device until it was in shards. He turned back to me and smiled for the first time. "This part is pretty low-tech," he said.

He picked up a small device and came around from behind the counter. "Raise your arms, please." I held out my arms and he scanned me from the top of my head to my shoes. Then, he waved the device over the Parrot. "Just need to be sure you're clean," he said, giving the Parrot a scratch under the chin. "Now swallow this."

He handed me a small, plasticky wafer, halfway between candy and machine. I looked at it.

"Biodegradable plastic," he said. "It will authenticate you to your transport and security at your destination. Then, it will dissolve in your small intestine. So, don't waste any time."

I shrugged and swallowed.

"Come on."

He walked to the front of the shop and turned an old-fashioned plastic sign over, so that the word "open" faced us. He walked back and did some complicated input to the store's system. A very low tone began to sound. "This way."

I picked up the Parrot and followed the man past the counter through a storage room and out a back door. We were on a large concrete pad; it would have been used for car parking back in the day. He took out his own mobile and swiped. "Your ride will be here in a minute."

"It's that easy?"

"Yes."

"How do you know they're not followed?"

He smiled again. "As I said, we're very low-tech. If they get this far, they've evaded capture. Here, they break the digital thread. There's no going back. Just forward."

"How many make it this far?"

He shrugged. "Maybe half."

"Did Miraluna Rose make it?"

"She made it. You'll find her at Refuge."

An unmarked private electric glided into the parking lot. "Here's your ride," the man said. "When you get to the jet, just get on. You'll get off at Refuge. It's all automated. Happy trails."

I knew I should liquidate him, to make sure we weren't followed. But I didn't. I hoped he had a lot more work to do. And besides, I don't do that.

* * *

A battered, nondescript Google took us to a small private jet field at the far edge of East Seattle. There was a single passenger drone parked there, and its lights flashed when I approached. The Parrot stretched up on my shoulder and flapped his wings.

"That's right," I told him. "It could be a long ride."

I settled into one of the four passenger seats and put the Parrot down on the floor. "Please stow all baggage," a recorded voice said. "No personal items can be on the floor during takeoff."

I picked him up, planted him on the seat next to me, and fastened the strap awkwardly around him. He *grawked* in protest. "Just for a few minutes."

The takeoff was smooth. No drones or surveillance planes. We headed east, then northeast. I entered a state of relaxed readiness. No idea how long the trip would be.

I was in a semi-hypnotic doze when the jet's automated voice came back on. "Finder! Finder!"

I came immediately alert.

"Dude! It's me. Can you hear me?"

"Librarian?"

"Solid!" I could hear the Librarian's intonation even through the flat modulations of the jet's announcement system.

"How are you doing this?"

"It was so easy. I followed your mobile to Seattle. When your signal stopped, I found a new node that came on the network at that exact location and time. I calculated nine-nines probability it was you. I followed it to the jetport and found a satellite overhead that showed only the one drone jet.

When your new signal began moving fast and then rose, it was obvious you were in that jet. So, I located the jet's specs and hacked into it. Easy!"

"Wait, my chip isn't encrypted?"

"Heck, yeah, it is. I am getting soooo awesome."

"You are awesome. Can you see my destination, Mr. Awesome?"

"No. But I'll stay on your signal and let you know any assumptions I can make. But that's not why I called."

"Why?" I reflexively dug my fingers into the nape of the Parrot's neck.

"I broke into some encrypted ReMe communications—about you."

"But they can't trace me, right? My mobile is gone. I swallowed a chip, but it should dissolve in a couple of hours."

"I dunno. I found you."

"Yeah, but you're awesome." I looked out the window. "Okay, I know where I am right now. The Area."

I looked down at a landscape uniformly covered with grey-green brush. The Area was a genetic modification project gone wrong. The government had been looking into alternatives for bioenergy and had planted a couple thousand acres in Idaho with a switchgrass/arundo reed hybrid. Well and good.

Then, they'd decided to mod the crop—because two years to harvest wasn't fast enough. Oops. The junk plant took off like green cancer, building impenetrable mats of rhizomes at the rate of a few feet a day. The stuff loved the semi-drought conditions in Idaho and Montana, and it was now making its way down into Colorado, mutating as it went. The scientists had thrown up their hands, and last they'd looked, the natural insecticides put out by the thousands of square miles of brush could slaughter a human in minutes.

"Way cool!" the Librarian said with the jet's voice. "What a brilliant place to hide an outlaw outpost."

"Except for the fact that it's toxic."

"Actually, not so much anymore. It's carcinogenic, but the actual level of toxic particulates in the air is"—a millisecond pause—"only 1.629 percent higher than in Laxangeles."

I sniffed, hoping the jet's filtration systems were good. "So, what were the ReMe comms about?"

"It was a delete order."

"As in execution?"

"Probably. ReMe likes to be all corporate."

"Well, they're not going to find me out here."

"Um, that's the thing."

"What?"

"They know where you're going."

"Oh." I chewed on that for a minute. I didn't come up with anything. I was miffed at all the banter before the Librarian had laid this on me. But then, it's not like there was anything I could do anyway. "Dobarro talked?"

"They made her. Listen," the Librarian said. "I've got a rock-hard encrypted comms channel set up for you. Memorize the address and when you get to Refuge, message me."

I listened to the string of numbers. I was using a physiomnemonic technique to tighten up the memory when the Librarian interrupted.

"Uh oh. Incoming."

"Where? I don't see anything." But then I did. Two black dots far in front of us. "Librarian! Can't you shoot them down with a satellite or something?"

"I wish, dude. But there's nothing overhead right now with that kind of weaponry."

I pulled the parachute out from under my seat and began shrugging it on.

"Dude," the Librarian said. "Are you okay?"

"Not really. But I could get lucky, right?" I opened my shirt and picked up the Parrot. I nestled him against my chest, legs splayed around me, and buttoned him in. I cinched the parachute around us both. There was a droning that came closer and closer. The black dots were helicopters, coming fast.

I watched them wheel up and toward us, calculating the angle that would take them within range of the drone. I felt the engine begin to lift, adjusting its course to avoid where the helicopters were now. But they were already someplace else, higher and closer. I could see the pilots. I could see mortar canons mounted underneath the carriage.

I moved to the emergency exit and put my hand on the door. If I could open the door and bail out at the exact instant they fired, it might work.

"Good luck, dude," the Librarian said. "Call me when you get there."

I exhaled slowly. I saw a flash of light.

* * *

I woke up on my back, sun blazing into my eyes. I was tangled up in vegetation; it was so thick, it was holding me up four feet above the ground, like a thick, lumpy mattress. The Parrot squirmed against my chest. There was a plume of smoke a good mile from my location, and the smell of burning plastic and fuel hung in the air. There was no sign of the black helicopters, and their drone was gone.

I took a stifled inhale of the air and then realized it was useless. I'd been breathing it the whole time I'd been unconscious. Besides, it would have killed the Parrot fast. It smelled kind of good, actually. Rich and vegetal and alive.

I uncinched the parachute rigging and the Parrot wriggled free. I put a warning hand on his back. "Stay close. Let's look around."

I saw my gear bag tangled in brush a few yards away and grabbed at it reflexively as I scrambled. But no water.

The mattress of shrub gave as I shrugged free and wormed my way to the ground, holding the Parrot to shield him from scratches. The ground was lumpy with rhizomes, dry and warm. The Parrot seemed unhurt—and eager to stretch his wings. I let him go.

And that's pretty much how I ended up here, hacking through the brush.

CHAPTER 16

Night fell. All I could do was keep heading in the direction the jet had been going. Refuge was probably miles away. It was probably hopeless.

When it got too dark to see, I wormed my way into the gaps between the bottoms of the reeds. The Parrot settled next to me. It was like a very tight nest. The rhizomes held the heat of the day, and they'd insulate us from the chill of the night. An astringent green odor rose up around us. It wasn't bad. Maybe it wouldn't poison us.

It was too bad, because the Parrot could probably make it out of here. If he'd leave me. Maybe if I bought it first, he'd figure it was okay to save himself. I fell asleep, the Parrot nestled against me, knowing this was probably where it all ended.

* * *

I woke a little after dawn to the sound of a motor thrumming in the distance. If it was ReMe's men coming to finish me off, at least I wouldn't have to spend another day hacking through the brush. I just lay there, listening to the motor. I was too exhausted to move. A dehydration headache thrummed my brain.

The Parrot *greeped* softly.

"Shush," I told him, but it didn't really matter. They'd have scopes and infrared and sensors and stuff. They'd find us.

As the vehicle came closer, I heard a whacking sound along with the noise of the motor. Whatever it was, it was getting through the shrubs, no problem. It got loud, and small rocks began pinging around in the air above me. I put my hand over the Parrot's head and curled my body around him, waiting for them to begin firing.

A fog of dust and ground-up vegetation filled the air. The vehicle made a wide circle around us and then stopped. Still no shots. I thought about slitting the Parrot's jugular with my laser knife and then doing my own. But a woman's voice rang out.

"Hey! You're safe. You can come out. We're from Refuge."

I uncurled myself from on top of the Parrot. He gurgled and rustled his wings. I held onto him, though. I wanted to show myself first, just in case.

I painfully rose up onto my knees. I still couldn't see above the shrubs, so I carefully craned my neck, fighting off a wave of dizziness.

Two ArcoTypes faced me from a hundred yards away, riding in what looked like an old-fashioned electric pickup truck.

"It's okay, buddy." I let go of the Parrot and he flew up, making a labored circle around the women and their vehicle.

They were less outré than some of their sisters. One was over six feet tall and extremely lean, with glossy black hair down to her waist, held back with a leather thong. The other was shorter and rounder, with amber hair that waved around a broad, strong face. They were both striking, with subtle signs of their mixed heritages.

They swiveled their heads to follow the Parrot's flight.

"Beautiful," the black-haired one said.

The amber-haired one held up her fist, and the Parrot landed on it. She laughed. "Little brother," she said to him. "Welcome." She looked at me. "You, too. Big brother." Both of them laughed at that.

I wasn't ready to smile. I was exhausted, dehydrated, bruised, and crabby. "Got any water?" I croaked. Fuck politeness.

The women looked concerned. "Oh, of course, I'm so sorry," the black-haired one said, pulling up a canteen and holding it out to me.

I trudged the distance to their vehicle, swimming through the reeds. The vegetation didn't seem as recalcitrant as it had yesterday. In fact, except for the extreme toughness of the branches and the pungent smell, it wasn't that different from normal brush. I must have been more delirious that I'd realized the day before.

The amber-haired woman held her cupped hand out to the other, who filled it with water. She put it to the Parrot's face. He drank and drank. It made me less crabby to see it.

I took the canteen and drained it. I felt bad, but I really needed it. The dizziness subsided a bit.

"I'm Rajendra," the dark-haired woman said. Her beautiful eyes were round, with irises almost as dark as the pupils.

"Nina," said the other, now stroking the Parrot's head. He *gurgled* in pleasure.

"I'm Finder."

Rajendra laughed. "Well, you found us."

They both seemed so *nice*. It wasn't something you saw much of these days—and nothing I'd picked up from any of the other ArcoTypes I'd met. Maybe that's what freedom did for them.

"What's his name?" Nina asked, cocking her head at the Parrot.

No one had ever asked that. "Uh. He doesn't have one."

"He doesn't have a name? How can that be? What do you call him?"

"He's just the Parrot." I shrugged.

"But what are you doing here?" Rajendra asked. "Your jet authenticated to us."

"But you're not one of us," Nina added.

"We thought we were retrieving bodies. We saw your jet flame out."

"Yeah. ReMe. I was coming to warn you."

"Motherfucker," Rajendra snarled, changing instantly from warm to outrage. "And you led them right to us."

"Back off. I used your supposedly secure pipeline all the way."

She frowned. "We've been breached."

"Yeah. It was Dobarro."

"Jane? You're lying."

"She was probably tortured. ReMe took her yesterday. That's why I came."

Nina burst into tears. Rajendra put an arm around her. I could tell she was fighting tears herself. The Parrot picked up on their angst and flew back onto my shoulder. It felt good to have him there.

"We've got to get back to Refuge right away."

I hoisted myself aboard their vehicle, letting the Parrot fly up himself. My body was trashed. I wedged into the rear seat of the cab. It had been stripped down to simple metal benches. Rugged and utilitarian. The front was mounted with some kind of threshing device that let it beat through the shrubbery. I could see a long trail of stubble leading in the direction of the bluff.

Rajendra wheeled the truck in a 180 and headed toward the distant rocks. The vegetal smell of ripping brush was thick in the air. Pebbles pinged against the thresher in a steady thrum.

Nina handed me a small jug. "Energy," she shouted over the noise of the engine and the shredding brush. "Good for you and your bird. The Parrot." She laughed again. "I know. I'm going to call him Griffon."

I cringed. It sounded stupid. "I just call him the Parrot."

She ignored me. "Hey, Griffon. Griffie." The Parrot didn't seem to mind. While Rajendra looked grim, Nina seemed unconcerned about the possibility of a ReMe attack.

It was a bumpy ride, but I used the lid of the jug to give the Parrot as much of the energy drink as I could. Then I slugged back a lot of the liquid, which was thick and sweet. I felt it doing good things inside me.

"Do you have comms?" I yelled.

"Are you crazy?" Rajendra yelled back. "You already brought ReMe here."

"I told you. That wasn't me. But I have a secure channel to someone who can help us."

"Hah," Rajendra scoffed.

But Nina handed me a dusty mobile. I tapped in the address the Librarian had given me, and in a few seconds, I got a text chat window.

Librarian. You there?

Whoo hoooo. You made it.

We got rescued by some ArcoTypes. On the way to Refuge now.

You da man.

Can you see my location?

Yeah. And I see some structures about 3.7296 miles away. That must be Refuge.

Can you scope it out?

Yeah. No sign of movement.

My gut twisted. I asked Nina, "Are you in communication with Refuge?"

"No, not right now. We squelch our signals except for one random time each day."

I didn't show her what the Librarian had said. Just hoped.

We bounced along. The bluff loomed ahead. I could make out the dots of a couple of structures, brown as the desert itself. Rajendra was taking no care to be stealthy, just grinding straight toward the bluff. The brush had thinned a bit, but the thresher was still churning it up. The truck's thick tires rumbled over the flattened stalks, and the air was thick with dirt and leaf prickle.

"Should we scout it out?" I yelled up to her.

She shrugged back at me and shouted, "Why?"

"ReMe."

She tossed a hank of hair out of her eyes and narrowed them. "We just need to get there."

I thought about sending the Parrot, but he needed rest and nourishment. I didn't want him in danger unless it was critical. I waited for shots or another rocket.

The pickup ran up a track on the side of the bluff and switchbacked its way up to the top. No shots. No sign of the black helicopters or more serious muscle.

The structures I'd seen from the distance were simple adobes. And they were empty. Empty as in, no windows, no furnishings. They'd been swept by sand for decades, probably old homesteads abandoned back when The Area went bad. I looked questioningly at Nina. She smiled.

"Camouflage. Good, huh?"

Rajendra drove the truck through a double-wide doorway into one of the adobes. "Home," she said. She hopped out and we followed. My leg muscles burned as I unwound myself from the back seat. The Parrot fluttered up and hopped off, sniffing around, no doubt as glad as I was to be out of the truck.

Rajendra grabbed onto what looked like a pile of rubble in the corner of the building. It slid aside in one piece; it was the cover for a wooden stairway leading into the bluff. Good camouflage, indeed.

I followed her and Nina down. For the first 20 feet, the stairs went straight down. The sides were shored up with timbers like a mine shaft. The air chilled, and the stairs leveled out onto a landing.

I was looking out into a cavern, complete with stalactites and stalagmites. It was at least as large as a commercial jet hangar; rippled curtains of stone faded away into gloom. The area in front of the landing was lit by LED lamps riveted into the stone, throwing baroque shadows onto the walls. On the cavern's floor, areas had been cleared of stalagmites to make paths and flat areas holding ragged tents. There was no movement.

"Search party's back," Rajendra shouted with gusto. She seemed to have no fear that ReMe's minions might be lurking there.

At once, women's voices answered in a babble of relief and welcome. A group of women scrambled out of the tent furthest back in the cavern. I chuffed out a breath in relief, but then my heart sank. There were so few of them.

But there she was, last out of the tent but striding forward to lead the group toward us. Miraluna Rose. The green hair was wild with dust. In the dim light, I thought I could make out the opal fire of her skin. She was dressed in a cotton shirt, heavy pants, and boots. She was magnificent.

Rajendra clambered down the remaining flight of steps, and we followed her. She gave Miraluna Rose a brief but strong hug, and then Miraluna Rose's eyes turned to me.

"Black helicopters were here. Is this the one who gave away our location?" she growled.

"No," Rajendra replied. "He says he came to warn us. I think he's an ally."

CHAPTER 17

We gathered in the biggest tent. There were four camp chairs and a camp table. A thick plastic mat insulated us from the cave floor, and there was a small heater with a big solar battery mounted on it. A small LED lantern hung from the ceiling, casting shadows everywhere and making some of the women's weird eyes even weirder.

I took one of the chairs, Parrot on my lap, and Miraluna Rose sat across from me. In the surveillance video, I'd seen beauty, and wildness, and deep determination. In person, her presence hit me like a shock wave. There was so much more. I felt raw power married to a wise and loving intelligence. And some kind of scent. I kept inhaling, trying to pick it out from the welter of other body smells. It was like nothing I had ever smelled, but it made the cavities in my skull tingle. It was something I wanted to keep sniffing and sniffing.

But the Parrot didn't seem to feel it. He *grawked* nervously, shifting from foot to foot as she looked at us. I ran my hand over his head, trying to calm him. No wonder he was edgy. I couldn't imagine all the strange things he could smell.

The women who didn't have chairs lounged on the floor. One with obsidian skin and red eyes leaned back against another with orange skin and turreted eye sockets. They all watched the Parrot intently, fascinated and drawn to him.

An unearthly pale woman pushed aside the tent flap and entered with a jug and cups. She gave the Parrot water and me hot tea. They passed around protein bars and even withered apples. I ate an unseemly amount and made sure the Parrot had his fill. Then, I told my story.

* * *

When I'd finished, everyone looked at Miraluna Rose. She was silent for a while, eyes focused on some imagined distance. While we waited for her to speak, I took her in again. Her hands were rough from hard work, the greenish fingernails worn down and chipped. She was so thin now that she was almost haggard, but there was plenty of muscle and sinew under the skin. I understood what Pellissier had meant. She had barely spoken, but I believed in her.

I believed that if anyone could lead the ArcoTypes out of corporate bondage, it was her. But what could even she do with so little resources? I'd pictured Refuge as a rebel hideaway, with a cadre armed and ready to fight. Instead, I counted eleven women—and they seemed to be close to starving to death. I stroked the Parrot, scooted my chair a little closer to the heater and waited.

When Miraluna Rose finally spoke, all she said was, "ReMe will be here. The helicopters dropped something in the desert. Probably a beacon. We haven't found it yet."

I dug my fingers into the feathers on the nape of the Parrot's neck and kneaded the muscles. "The Parrot can find the beacon."

Miraluna Rose's eyes flashed. She was gorgeous. "No!" she said. "This is a refuge from slavery. We won't let you put the animal in danger."

"He's not my slave," I snapped, stung. "He's my partner."

She gave me a hard look and then held out her hand, offering herself to the Parrot. He sniffed her suspiciously, fluttered his wings, and then settled back into my lap. She shrugged. "Cloud," she said.

The woman with albino skin and eyes and a haze of white hair came over and knelt in front of me, face-to-face with the Parrot. He sniffed her and *snurkled*, easing down and meeting her gaze. I kept my hands quiet, letting the Parrot make his own decision. Cloud gazed at the Parrot, her face softening. They stayed that way for minutes, and then she said, "Yes."

Miraluna Rose's stern posture relaxed a bit, and I thought she looked at me with new respect. "Thank you," she said to the Parrot. "We appreciate your help. Both of you. Rajendra, stay up top with them until the mission is completed."

* * *

I took out the Parrot's harness pack and put it on him so that he'd be able to bring back what he found if it was small enough. We climbed back up the narrow wooden stairs into the adobe, the Parrot on my shoulder. We moved past the truck and stood in the doorway. I stroked the Parrot, nuzzled against his throat. This was the part of our relationship I always hated—sending him out alone.

I let him hop onto my arm and then held it up into the sky. "Find it," I told him. It was as much a prayer as an instruction.

We watched the blue dwindle into the sky.

"Does he know what he's looking for?" Rajendra asked.

"He'll find it."

"How?"

"I don't really know," I answered. "But he will."

We sat down inside the adobe, leaning our backs against the wall to wait. Rajendra looked peaceful, so I said, "I thought there would be more of you."

She frowned. "It's so difficult to bring us out here. And so dangerous. Not everyone makes it—and a lot of us are too afraid to try." Her black eyes filled with tears. "And some of our sisters have died once they made it to Refuge. It's harsh here."

I pictured a woman with the genes of a tropical creature shivering in the caves; a woman bred for desert heat or humid jungles succumbing to the cavern's chill.

"I'm sorry," I said. I felt it, but it sounded trivial.

Rajendra made a sound that was halfway between a sob and a scoff. Then, we were silent.

* * *

My eyes were raw from squinting at the sky when I finally saw the Parrot's shape, undwindling against the blue sky. He flew down and landed at our feet, panting. I felt a pang at his exhaustion. We'd been through a lot lately. I picked him up and held him against my chest and then cradled him in one arm as I felt his pack. There was something in his chest pocket. He'd done it. I knew he would.

I followed Rajendra back down into the cavern, carrying the Parrot. She called out as we hit the landing, and women gathered again in front of the main tent. Miraluna Rose stepped out and motioned us all in. I took the same chair and laid the Parrot's booty on the table. It was a small white orb. Clearly a location beacon.

Miraluna Rose nodded. "It's been broadcasting for what? Thirteen hours? They could be here any time."

"Let's get rid of it in any case," Rajendra said.

"Right. Take it out and smash it good. Get all the chips. Then bring it back."

Rajendra took the beacon away. We looked at Miraluna Rose. She looked at me. She held out her hand again to the Parrot, but he backed away with a little *grawp*.

"It's probably the cat," I said. "He's bird and dog."

She shrugged. "Too bad. I'd like to hold him."

"He's our little brother," Nina piped up. "We've never had an ArcoType who didn't have some human in him," she said to me.

That rankled me. "He's not an ArcoType. He's just a chimera. No brand name, no patent, no intellectual property."

"Where did he come from?" Miraluna Rose asked.

"I made him."

"Why?"

"Just to be with me."

"Hmph," was all she said.

I felt it again—the uneasy way I now felt about the Parrot. It made me want to earn these women's trust all the more.

We sat there, mostly silent, waiting for Rajendra to return. The women all wanted to touch the Parrot. He sat on the ground, enjoying the attention, although he shied away from some of them. He seemed to like Nina the best. I wondered if it was something about her complex biochemistry or just her sweetness. Meanwhile, my mind was working. We had to get out of here.

We had heard Rajendra stomping down the stairs, and a few moments later, she scrambled back into the tent, holding out shards of plastic and metal in her hand. "It's done."

All the women's eyes turned back to Miraluna Rose. But I spoke first. "We have to go," I said.

"Where? How?" she answered.

I didn't have a plan. All I had was the Librarian, but I was beginning to believe he could do anything. "I have a friend who might be able to send us a jet."

Miraluna Rose looked suspicious. "Who is he?"

"He's an AI."

"An AI? Where is it located?"

"Everywhere. And it's *he*, not *it*. You should know that. Let me use your comms and I'll contact him."

Miraluna Rose exchanged a glance with another woman, one whose head, neck, and arms rippled with soft, brown hair. "I guess a comms lockdown doesn't matter anymore," she said. The brown-haired woman dug a ruggedized mobile out of the pocket of her coveralls and held it out to me.

I tapped in the address for the Librarian's encrypted channel. He came right up.

Dude! I was worried. Your signature disappeared over the Area.

We made it. I'm at Refuge.

Oh, wow. Is it rad?

I saw Miraluna Rose wince at the Librarian's surfer lingo. I shrugged.

Not exactly. We need transport out of here. In the next few hours. Can you handle that?

How many?

Twelve, plus the Parrot.

I dunno. You'd need a commercial jet for that.

There was the typical blink-of-an-eye pause while the Librarian scanned the networks.

I can get a jet there for you, but it won't be clean.

What do you mean?

There will be fingerprints of the hijack. Maybe traceable back to me. Definitely tagged as illegal. You'll probably get arrested when you land. Can you deal with that?

This time, my own thought process took only slightly longer than his.

We can deal. But what about you?

Dude! I'm in. Let's fuck up the man.

Now, I had to pause. If the Librarian got fingered, they'd wipe his memory.

You sure about this?

Dude, I'm a warrior. Yeah.

Rajendra looked at me with contempt. "So, we'll end up right back in ReMe's hands? I'd rather die here."

Miraluna Rose looked more sorrowful. "I'm afraid she's right," she said to me. "Law enforcement is practically ReMe's private security. If we go back, we'll be turned over as property." She looked around the tent, meeting the eyes of each woman in turn. "Sisters. Stay and fight, or go?"

The lounging women got to their feet. They were charged up.

"Fight!

"Fight!"

"I'm ready to die."

"Right now!"

The Parrot, excited, flew up and began *skronking*.

I raised my voice. "Wait. There's another way."

They stared at me, fiery-eyed; their smell was suddenly intense. The Parrot landed on Nina's shoulder and began nuzzling her hair. She put up a hand to stroke him.

"There's more than one way to fight," I said. "I've got a gun, but it won't do us much good. You have a much bigger weapon—Pellissier and Adnomyx."

"Clarissa tried. She created Refuge," said Miraluna Rose. "And the Maxman Institute. She tried, but she couldn't protect us."

"And now ReMe is coming to wipe us out," Rajendra said.

"Clarissa is beautiful," Nina said.

"She loves us," said a woman with the eyes of a hawk.

Rajendra scowled. "So what?

"She's one of the most powerful people in the world," I said.

"She's not," Rajendra spat. "Her sick son keeps her weak."

I thought about the boy, Cornell. Her huddling in with him and the Cousins, hoping for some cure. "She's not weak," I said. "Maybe the boy has distracted her, kept her from seeing the obvious."

"What's that?"

"Adnomyx can talk directly to probably 85 percent of the people on the planet. And it has software algorithms that can find the people who will support you. ReMe has kept you hidden. It's time to introduce yourselves to the world—your way."

Miraluna Rose looked troubled. "We have no legal standing."

"There's something more powerful than the law," I said. "Entertainment."

The comm channel to the Librarian was still open.

We need to get out of here soon

I know. I've been working on it. It's hard, even for me.

Can you do it?

I'm thinking a military transport helicopter.

What? That seems impossible, even for you.

I've got a friend.

There was something funny there, something human that I couldn't quite parse.

She's an AI that controls military defense for the Western region.

She. That was interesting, but I held my tongue. I didn't want to embarrass him.

You are truly amazing. How long will it take for her to get it to us?

Two hours and 37.380 seconds.

Do it. And then patch me through to Pellissier. And thank you.

I always got your back, dude.

* * *

It was a good five minutes before Pellissier came on, with video. She was in her office; she looked exhausted. "Where are you?"

"I'm at Refuge."

"You made it."

"Yes, but ReMe is on its way."

"Jane is dead."

"I'm so sorry."

"I know she was brave."

"I know it, too. But now we need your help. Fast."

"What? Anything."

I could feel the women around me, tense, afraid, and defiant.

"We're coming home. And we need you to prepare a welcome for us."

CHAPTER 18

The very mystified but extremely professional flight crew delivered us to Monterrey as a pink, pollution-painted sky was fading to dusk.

My bones ached from the jarring ride, and the Parrot was limp in my lap. A couple of the women were practically spitting with tension. It felt very good to be out of the desert.

A squad of military police was assembled in formation on the tarmac, weapons at the ready. Pellissier was there, too, ducking her head against the wind from the copter blades.

Miraluna Rose had been calm and commanding during the flight, reassuring the others. But when she saw Pellissier, she started up and tears stood in her eyes. "Oh," was all she said, but it was more of a gasp.

Next to Pellissier was a tall man with some complicated electronic gear over half his face. And, dancing around in the wind, mobiles held high, were a man and a woman in the kind of clothing and gear worn by the rich and fashionable. They were both heavily modded, and I could see digital implants in the woman's forehead.

Then my view of the tarmac was blocked by our transport's pilot. His professionalism was now tinged with menace. "I'm under orders to let you out the door one at a time, where you'll be taken into military custody." He pointed to Rajendra, sitting nearest the door. "You first."

We filed out, me and the Parrot last. The soldier who helped me down gave a wary glance at him, but only said, "Hold onto it."

The squad of MPs herded us into a ragged circle, the bedraggled and filthy women still looking wild and dangerous, the soldiers stiff with tension, trying hard not to stare.

The two fashion victims were moving around us, dancing on their toes, squatting down to get different angles with their devices. The woman had a semi-pro VR recorder with a long boom mike that she kept trying to pass over the heads of the soldiers encircling us.

The squad leader said, "Forward—"

"Wait right there!" It was Pellissier's gearhead, rushing forward and waving a legal device.

"These…people are under arrest. They've diverted military assets; that's a federal crime," the head MP said.

"No, they are immigrants seeking political asylum," Pellissier's gearhead responded.

The MP snorted. "Who are you?"

"I'm Jeremiah Sato, head of legal affairs for Adnomyx."

The soldier looked impressed but unmoved. "You'll have to go through channels. My orders are to remand these people into custody now."

The lawyer waved his device in the soldier's face—and the fashion guy waved his own device in front of the lawyer's, whispering urgently into his headset.

"This is a formal request for asylum, already filed with the Ninth Circuit Court," the lawyer said.

"You'll have to go through channels. Forward march!"

As we walked toward the row of buildings next to the hangars, I watched Miraluna Rose. She kept her eyes on Pellissier as long as she could. And Pellissier looked back at her just as avidly.

* * *

The military treated us well enough. They searched us, confiscating my gear bag and a couple of knives the women had. They took the few mobiles among us, and then they herded us onto a bus, four MPs with rifles drawn at the back, four more in the front. It was windowless, climate-controlled, and lit by LEDs in the ceiling. A soldier had tried to take the Parrot as I climbed aboard, but when I told him he was a comfort bioid, he backed right off.

I itched to access my comms and check in with the Librarian, but otherwise, I felt fine about taking a break. I was still worn out by my overland trek to Refuge, and the Parrot was probably in worse shape. I got my own cell, a very clean, featureless room with an adequate bed and even a bathroom with a small shower stall. I got into the shower with the Parrot and stayed in there a long time. Fuck the military's water ration. The Parrot and I both slept like dogs.

And we were out the next day. A soldier came to my room, rifle at ease, to take me through the release process. I exited into a large waiting room to find Pellissier, Sato, the lawyer, and the two fashionistas, along with most of the women.

Pellissier, Miraluna Rose, and the lawyer were standing, heads tipped in toward each other, listening to the lawyer talk. Rajendra and the fashionista I'd started thinking of as Fashion Boy were huddled in a couple of chairs. He was speaking to her softly and rapidly, Rajendra speaking more slowly in reply to his questions, his mobile held between them.

The modded-up woman rushed up to me, brandishing her mobile. "You're the one who rescued them, right? Why did you do it? What is that on your shoulder? A bird? Who are you, anyway? Oh, yeah, say your name for my viewers."

I looked her over. She was actually a young girl, a teenager. But she had the extensive mods you're supposed to be at least eighteen to get. She had one digital implant above each eye. They looked like wide-angle recorders; they'd pick up whatever she saw. She'd had her ears clipped into little points, and they were studded with more tiny devices that looked like sensors. A jewel embedded in the hollow of her throat flickered red in time with her voice.

"Who are you?" I asked.

"Oh!" She sounded surprised I didn't know. "I'm Cookie Clane. I'm an Influencer!"

This was some of Pellissier's good work. Millions of people followed the media and social channels of Influencers. Cookie Clane could spread the ArcoTypes' story around the world.

"I'm the Finder," I said. "This is the Parrot. But you should talk to that woman with the green hair over there."

"I did! She's amazing. I already posted our interview—and tons of memes. But she said that you were the one who rescued them."

I thought a moment. I wanted to give her something simple and shareable—that would take me out of the spotlight. "Miraluna Rose is the leader of these women who freed themselves from slavery. All I did was get them transportation."

"Oooh," said Cookie. "Checkit! Can I pet your bird?"

"No."

"But I've got to stream him." She moved around the Parrot, mobile held up close to him, babbling a steady stream of commentary.

The last of the women filed through the door, and we hopped an Adnomyx drone, the two Influencer kids buzzing around us all the way.

* * *

We landed at the back of the Adnomyx campus and went in the same door I'd used when I came to get the Parrot back. Everything was as cool and orderly as the last time. The vestibule with its wooden curios, and on into the big room where the clones still reclined, as though they'd never moved.

Pellissier led us in, the women looking around with curiosity and a bit of awe. I wondered what circumstances some of them had come from.

And there was Roh Maxman, enthroned in the same chair in which I'd last seen her. Maxman gave me the evil eye, and I gave it right back to her. Pellissier rushed over to kiss her, and the other women followed. They also kissed her, one by one, calling her Matriarch. They acted like she was their queen or something.

Cornell, Pellissier's little boy, came in, holding the hand of a minder. His skin had even more of a bluish tinge. There are some things that neither science nor love can heal. He climbed into her lap and rested his head against her chest. Her hand came up to stroke his wispy hair.

I sat down and let the Parrot go. Sato, looking slightly aghast himself, sat down near me. His one uncovered eye looked over at me. I shrugged.

After each ArcoType greeted Maxman, she went over to the clones and hugged and kissed them. The clones clucked and chuckled softly. They seemed to love being held. The Parrot followed them over there and got right in the middle of it all. He climbed into laps, glorying in being stroked and scratched.

The Influencer kids whirled around, squealing with excitement as they streamed the bizarre scene.

I watched with a bit of amazement as these feral refugees became sweet and soft. They nestled among the clones or sat at Maxman's feet, gazing up at her with love. The air was alive with woman smell, not the tang I'd smelled in the cave but something honeyed and soothing. I could almost see the old lady as Pellissier had described her, not a whack job but just someone searching for connection.

They settled slowly, the Parrot still wandering among them, begging for more touch. A side of him I hadn't seen.

Pellissier swiped her mobile, and an assistant came in carrying a box of new mobiles. She walked around the room handing them out. I quickly authenticated mine, noticing that it was a top-of-the-line Xiaomi. Then I switched it off without looking at messages. I was too tired.

Everyone was fiddling with their new mobiles, while the Influencers used their devices to stream everyone else looking at their new devices. I assumed Xiamoi had paid for the privilege of being part of all this. Advertising. Why not?

Then Miraluna Rose spoke up.

"It's time to get to work." She looked at Sato. "Any news about the asylum request?" It was Pellissier's headquarters and Pellissier's money, but Miraluna Rose had immediately taken command.

Sato touched the side of the apparatus that covered half his face and said, "Nothing so far. The filing got you out of custody, but I had to guarantee you'd stay here at Adnomyx. Not exactly house arrest, but…"

"There's nowhere else I'd rather be right now," Miraluna Rose said. She was so calm; not frozen, just utter stillness. Then I saw a single shiver pass across her skin, like a gust of wind on water. I wanted to feel that flutter against the palm of my hand. I hated the desire.

A sleek assistant brought in water and snacks in delicate bowls. She was followed by an angular man with ebony skin and golden eyes carrying a large mobile screen. He wore a more deluxe version of the lawyer's pricey suit, and he'd decorated his face with a few thin lines of gold. I eyed him, looking for the traces of exotic DNA that would reveal him as an ArcoType, but didn't see them. I decided he was simply an extraordinarily beautiful human.

Pellissier got up to greet him. I was astonished to see her hug him—and he hugged back. "This is David Babangida," she said. "My chief data scientist."

Babangida looked around, seemingly unperturbed by the chaos of females. "Hello, everyone." He walked up to Maxman, lifted her hand and held it briefly. Maxman looked up at him with eyes that didn't seem to focus.

"David, what have you got for us so far?"

It was Pellissier who spoke, but Babangida instinctively replied to Miraluna Rose. "I sliced and diced our global consumer database in a few ways, looking for affinity groups. I began, of course, with basic demographics. But that's just the baseline. I added in micro-geographies, media consumption habits and preferences. Our preferences data is *extremely* deep," he added, looking extremely smug.

He swiped his screen and held it up for us to look at. "I weighed all this against psychographic data—that's really the most predictive—and I came up with five custom audiences that are most likely to have affinity for our messaging."

I looked around the room. I'd gotten the gist; I was used to sifting through big data, although not as big data sets as Adnomyx's. Most of the women looked edgy and restless. Miraluna Rose looked intent, like she was trying to absorb all this. The Influencers were staring at their mobiles. The clones were in their gaga place. Pellissier seemed extremely pleased, so evidently Babangida was on the right track.

Babangida brandished his mobile. "I named the custom segments Fiery and Furry, Primal Connectors, Goddess Wranglers, Pan-species Panegyric, and Beyond Human."

Miraluna Rose looked a bit stunned. "These names are...what?"

Pellissier was smiling now. "They're groups of people—all over the world—who share the kinds of attitude and beliefs that will put them on our side."

Suddenly Maxman croaked from her chair, "My church. The New Church of the Expansive Essence?"

Nina jumped up and went over to her, taking her hand and looking adoringly into the crumpled face. "What, Matriarch?"

"The New Church. Expansive..." Her voice wound down to a mumble.

"The Matriarch wants us to found a church," Nina said breathlessly.

Pellissier spoke up. "No, actually, she just means—"

But the other women ignored her, crowding up around Maxman, stroking her arms, holding her feet, grabbing for her hands. The Influencers followed, greedily sucking it up with their mobiles. "Tell us!" the women begged. "Tell us what we should do."

The attention woke the old woman up and she sat up straighter. But before she could speak, Miraluna Rose stood up, and everyone's eyes automatically went to her. She was magnetic. Her skin glowed with internal light that seemed to infuse her with authority. "The Matriarch has spoken," she said firmly. "Now, David Babangida will tell us how to carry out what she's told us to do."

That was very nicely done, I thought. Leadership, indeed. I looked around for the Parrot. He was wandering around the perimeter of the room, snuffling. He'd turn into a real dog if I wasn't careful.

"How many people are in each of your segments?" Miraluna Rose asked.

"Anywhere from a few hundred thousand to a million or so."

She looked doubtful.

"It's plenty," Babangida said. He picked up his lecture where he'd left off. "Within our custom segments, I've further segmented them according to influence on the different socials." At the word "influence," both of the modded fashionistas looked up and then immediately went right back to their mobiles. "Our proprietary algorithms have determined the best cadence for release of content and messaging. We've already contacted a few key influencers in different channels. After giving the first exclusive access to Cookie and Kyrell here."

At the sound of their names, the two Influencer kids brightened up and popped to attention.

"My meme of Miraluna Rose is blowing up right now," said Fashion Boy, as I still thought of him.

"My live stream of the arrest was picked up by WCNN," said Cookie, obviously trying to top Kyrell.

"You're our media vanguard," Babangida told them. "We'll keep providing you and the other top Influencers with exclusive content, and we'll support the earned media with ad buys. Just tell us what you need."

"I need a case of Icelandic Ice water," Cookie said.

"Sushi," Kyrell said. "And organic fruit."

I raised an eyebrow. Those were big asks, even for media stars. Babangida looked at Pellissier, who nodded, and swiped his screen. "It's on the way," he said. "Meanwhile, relax, get to know each other." The Influencers began chattering to the ArcoTypes, capturing it all with their mobiles. Kyrell plopped down next to the woman with the turreted eyes, fascinated. "Do you see differently than we do?" I heard him ask. "What do I look like?"

The next couple of hours were a blur of media. They hauled in a couple of huge screens and a VR broadcast setup, and Miraluna Rose began doing interviews. It started with indie operations, Influencer kids and wannabes streaming to their fans. It wasn't long before the first meme went gliral on the socials. When something goes viral and global at the same time, you know it's unstoppable. It was Miraluna Rose staring into the distance, looking radiant, saying, "Bioluminescence feels like an orgasm running through your veins."

I wondered if that was true. Or if she was just naturally good at media stuff, too.

Then, the mainstream media caught on. BuzzFeed, UtMo$t, WashPo, and the like did remotes while they scrambled to get reporters live onsite.

Adnomyx techs had set up a large screen to track the global mentions, hashtags, and memes. #FreedomNotIP. #NobodyOwnsMe. #WhatIsHuman? I watched tweets and headlines scroll down the side of the screen while the four newscasters on split screens talked excitedly. Behind a thin woman newsreader with hair skinned back in a tight bun, a larger-than-life image of Miraluna Rose appeared. Her wild hair and glittering eyes diminished the merely human woman in front of her, making her seem like a cheap knockoff.

The analytics included a heat map showing where the most activity was. I watched as the coast of California went from yellow to orange to red. There were red-hot spots in major population areas all over the world. Kinshasa, Fuzhou, Izmir lighting up with the buzz.

Ubers, passenger drones, and commercial vehicles began to arrive, disgorging manic media whores, many of them as heavily modded as Cookie and Kyrell.

I watched Pellissier's assistant, Tay, confer with her. He pointed to the Cousins, still lolling on their divan, indifferent to the growing excitement. Pellissier shrugged. She looked feverishly happy.

Soon Tay was back with the first media group. They strutted in, all glossy fabric and shiny electronics, each with an assistant or two trailing along with more gear. I watched as each paused and struck a pose, waiting to be recognized. The ArcoTypes mostly ignored them.

At first, Tay tried to keep control, herding them over to his boss. But they became immediately distracted by the outrageously ornamental ArcoTypes, barely noticing Pellissier's subtle beauty. They rushed off in all directions, electronics held out.

There was a flurry of activity at the door, and a wave of silence spread into the room as an auburn-haired man strode in. Even I recognized him. Keeshawn LeRoy, the most famous and influential news whore in the world. He'd paid his dues as an Influencer in the smaller socials, put in time with the mainstream media by reporting on politics for Amazon, and then moved on to global celebrity status when a sex VR he'd made with the prime minister of India had been leaked.

Babangida popped up and rushed over to him. I could see he wanted to hug LeRoy but held himself back. The news whore accepted his welcome with the glamorous grace of someone accustomed to being the most important person in the room. He looked around, taking in Pellissier and Cornell, the clones, the ArcoTypes and the media kids, me and Sato sitting on the edges, with an expression of disgusted glee. He thought he outclassed all of us.

"I'm going to need a separate room," he said imperiously. "And quiet. And then bring me Miraluna Rose." Babangida and Tay scrambled.

I gathered the Parrot in my arms and went to sit next to Pellissier. Her cheeks and neck were flushed pink under her pearly powder.

"I can't believe they're here," she said. "Look at them."

I looked.

"They're amazing," I said. "You did what you set out to do."

She sighed. "We have such a long way to go. Jeremiah says the litigation could take years."

Sato plopped down on the other side of her, in time to hear our conversation. He laughed. "You've already won. They've won. Keeshawn LeRoy is bigger than the President. The ArcoTypes belong to the media now—and it's much more powerful than the law."

My job was done. Not Thin Man's job, but the job I'd wanted to do.

I was tired, and I hadn't had any drugs in a couple of days. I gathered up the Parrot—I had to drag him from the middle of a pile of clones, ArcoTypes, and media kids. He *skritched* in protest, but then settled himself in my arms. He was tired too, I could tell.

I looked around. Should I say goodbye? Pellissier, Sato, and Miraluna Rose were deep in conversation, bent over Sato's screen. Nina was speaking earnestly to a kid with skin dyed blue and prosthetic horns implanted in his forehead. In fact, the only way I could tell he wasn't an ArcoType was by his elaborate streaming rig. And Rajendra seemed to be in a trance, sprawled among the clones, head thrown back and eyes closed.

I gave Roh Maxman one more evil look and slipped out the door.

I hopped a Google, told it to go back to Berkeley, and opened the comms on my shiny new mobile.

A video message from Thin Man, looking tweaked to the point of stroke. "Okay, you fucked me," his video image snarled. "But you'll never work again." I deleted it.

A voice message from the Librarian. "Dude! I can't believe you don't leave your comms on. How are people supposed to get in touch with you? Call me!"

I tapped to respond and the Librarian was immediately there. He was practically panting with excitement. Which was interesting. He seemed to be becoming more and more emotional.

"Dude!"

"Dude. How's it hanging, meathead?"

"We totally did it, didn't we?"

"You were amazing," I said. "Hijacking military transport? And what about this AI friend of yours?"

"She's just a friend," he said, a little too hastily.

I did not want to pry but I was deeply curious about how two artificial intelligences got together. All I said was, "A very good friend to have."

"So why are you going home? Don't you want to be there?"

The Librarian's enthusiasm made me realize just how tired I was. "The ArcoTypes are in very good hands. Clarissa Pellissier has plenty of resources—and I don't do that well in groups."

"I thought you and Clarissa might have a thing going on. You'd be good together. A real power couple."

"Oh, grow up," I said. "I'll talk to you tomorrow."

CHAPTER 19

My shop had a chilly air of abandonment, although I hadn't been away that long. The Parrot ran in and sniffed all over. Then he sat up straight by the refrigerator, his feed-me-now posture.

"Really? You ate a bunch at Adnomyx."

Really. It must be a reflex, seeing the refrigerator for the first time in a while. I shrugged and pulled out seaweed, cricket powder, some cooked rice, and a carrot. The rice was spoiled, which was a shame. But there was fermented tofu to make up for it.

"We're back to crickets and seaweed," I told him. "No more of that luxe stuff they serve at Adnomyx."

The Parrot didn't seem to mind. He tucked into his meal with gusto.

I headed for my drugs. Food could wait. I gave myself a B-12 shot; I was tempted by the testosterone, but I was headed for sleep. A long one. I made up my stack. The phenibut, picamilon, and L-theanine. The CBD drops and progesterone. Then I snorted a little morphine, just to make sure my body got the message.

I picked up the Parrot and juiced him with some B-12, too. He *skreeped* a little, but took it well. He was tired too.

The water recycler was empty, so I ordered a case of my favorite, Heart of Harbin. I deserved it. I added my standard food order, plus a piece of fresh halibut. Me and the Parrot would eat that for breakfast.

I took him up on the roof to poop. The sky over the hills was already plum. To the west, a bitter sun hit the horizon. The hot breeze felt good. Then I felt my meds begin to kick in. I barely made it to my bed.

* * *

I woke up in fetal position with the Parrot curled into the nook made by the backs of my knees. I rolled over and worked my fingers through the ruff on his neck, feeling what it was like to be home.

I turned on all my screens—before food, before drugs, before pissing. The socials were buzzing about the ArcoTypes. Photos, images, and memes scrolled by. On the UtMo$t feed, a news whore was being made over by a stylist, who was adding extravagant colors to her skin and gluing jewels along her eyebrows to mimic an ArcoType's beauty.

It was like aliens had landed, I thought, and then realized that they pretty much had.

I deleted all my messages without scanning them. I'd call the Librarian later, and there was no one else I wanted to talk to except the Parrot.

He was whimpering for his breakfast, so I unwrapped the halibut, dusted it with galangal and salt, and put it in the frying pan. I kept an eye on it while I downed my morning stack, feeling my brain come back alive.

The Parrot scarfed his meal down in seconds. "Slow down, buddy," I told him. "That's primo stuff." But that's a dog, isn't it? I tried to make my fish last as long as I could, and then I licked the plate.

Miraluna Rose was in the middle of a livestreamed Ask Me Anything. I brought it up on my big screen. She was clean and groomed. She was wearing a silvery gray dress, cut simply, with cap sleeves that showed off the tight muscles of her arms. The silver color brought out the greenish sheen of her skin. Her eyes were outlined in metallic silver and green; her lips were painted a cool lavender pink. She looked like a goddess.

She was sitting relaxed and regal on an orange upholstered chair. That bugged me. Blue would have been better. Or gray, something neutral to contrast with her skin. A middle-aged man with the look of the tech elite was sitting next to her, watching her admiringly as she spoke. I tapped his face on the screen. He was the CEO of Joven Media, the company that had bought Reddit a few years ago.

A super appeared on the screen, showing the next question: Do you feel unique?

I saw her smile slightly. Stupid question. But then, they would be, mostly.

"I really just feel like myself," she said. "Don't we all feel that way? I understand that I'm different—but that's mostly when I'm around...regular people."

Good answer. She shouldn't say "humans," with the implication the she and the rest of the ArcoTypes aren't. Sato had said that was the key message they had to hit over and over, that the ArcoTypes were human.

The next question appeared: What do you plan to do if you get your freedom?

I saw a flash of anger pass across her face, but she quickly brought it back to the calm, noble expression.

"I am free right now," she said. "No matter what the government thinks."

How do you feel about your owner?

"Nobody can own another person."

Your kidnapper, then?

"ReMe was engaged in illegal business practices. We're counting on the legal system to do what's right—for us and society."

Is it true that the two of you are going to reunite on Keeshawn LeRoy's show?

"Absolutely not."

Were you in love with him? Is he in love with you?

I could see the color leave her face, even in the video lighting. I wondered what her blush would look like. Then, she smiled.

"I know this is an AMA. But I'm not going to answer that."

Miraluna Rose was extraordinary. I could see what Pellissier meant. She was a natural leader. And she articulated the ArcoTypes' message with dignity. Was it really the synergy of her disparate DNA, or did the human embryo she came from contain all this at the start? It didn't matter.

There's only so much screenage I can take, and I could see that Pellissier and Miraluna Rose had things well under control. I took the Parrot up to the roof. Pearly smog cut the sun and cooled the air. While he snuffled around looking for the right spot, I called the Librarian.

"Hey, meathead."

"How's the *man?*"

"Still tired."

"We kicked *ass!*"

"I think you get most of the credit. Hey, how's your lady AI friend? Is she in trouble?"

"She's cool. They'll be parsing their data for a long time, trying to find out what happened with that transport."

"She took a big risk, didn't she? Is she going to be all right?"

"She'll be all right. She's crazy smart. She's altering the data faster than they can analyze it."

"I'm glad to hear it." I took a breath of Berkeley air, enjoying that feeling of having done something good. I watched the Parrot squeeze out a turd.

"Listen, Finder," the Librarian said. "The ArcoTypes are going to make huge waves. Society is going to change fast. I'm gonna get to the beach. I just know it."

"There's still a long legal case. Pellissier's got a good lawyer and plenty of coins, but ReMe will drag this out as long as possible."

"I don't think so," he said excitedly. "My predictive modeling says that ReMe will admit fault, negotiate down the penalties, and then sell its IP. I'm already putting together a consortium to buy it."

"You're always a step ahead, aren't you?"

"Actually, I'm usually seven steps ahead."

I laughed. "I'm ready to haul your half of a carcass down to the beach anytime you say."

"I'll let you know," the Librarian said. He was totally serious.

Chapter 20

I turned off all my screens again and had a good couple of days, just me and the Parrot. A weather inversion had lifted, and the air was remarkably cool and clear. I spent some time on the roof, lounging under a sunshade, the Parrot on my lap. I could get to like a lapdog.

Once again, I mass-deleted all my new messages on every channel. I'd start fresh. Sometime. I ate a lot and slept a lot.

I didn't check the news or the feeds. Clearly, Miraluna Rose and the rest of the ArcoTypes had captured the media and the socials. It could go two ways: Public opinion would demand freedom for the women. Or, all the buzz would act as free advertising, and ReMe would be overwhelmed with orders.

I figured the Librarian was probably right—he'd been right all the way so far. The charisma of Miraluna Rose combined with the market clout and messaging genius of Pellissier and Adnomyx would be incredibly difficult for the weaselly Niheloush and ReMe to beat.

I didn't need to follow every VR cast and feed to watch it play out.

On the morning of the third day since we'd been back at home, I was just beginning to think about getting some work done. Nothing heavy, just maybe browsing through some of the latest genome catalogs. The Parrot and I had eaten; my morning stack was kicking in nicely. Life was good.

The door sensor ponged, and the camera showed the scintillating green hair of Miraluna Rose.

I opened the door and she slid in out of the heat. The Parrot *greeped*. She went over to him, laughing. "Hello, Griffon." He nuzzled her hair briefly and then squawked, trying madly to get away. She let him go, and he flew to the top of my workbench, looking miffed and wiping his beak against his side.

Cat, I thought.

I moved back into the room, and she followed me. I just stood there, and she stood, composed, looking back at me. Her scent began to flow into the room. As her smell drifted toward me, it seemed like I could feel it settling on my skin, flaming it. I took a deep whiff of it and moved away.

"How did you get here? I thought you were under house arrest."

She shrugged. I watched phosphorescence travel across her skin. "Your friend the Librarian made it happen."

"He's pretty good, isn't he?"

"He's amazing. He's going to file an amicus brief for us." She settled herself on the couch.

"Would you like water?"

"That would be lovely."

I got a bottle of Harbin water out of the refrigerator and poured two glasses. I looked doubtfully at the Parrot. Usually, I'd share my glass with him. After I handed Miraluna Rose her glass, I reached for the Parrot, but he was still sulking. I sat down in the big chair across from her.

Miraluna Rose took a long swallow. I saw moisture bead her lips. "I've been trying to reach you," she said. "You seem to have all your comms turned off."

"Why?"

"I don't know why you'd turn off your comms."

I felt slow and stupid with her. "No, why did you want to contact me?"

She smiled. "I wanted to see how you were. I thought you'd come back."

"To Adnomyx?"

"Yes."

"Why?"

"I wanted you to come back."

My stomach flipped. My groin caught fire. This was terrible. Could she tell? I took three deep breaths.

"Why are you here?" I said again, even more stupidly.

"I wanted to thank you and ask you to join us."

"You need lawyers and news whores. You don't need me." Still, I felt a pang of longing.

She shrugged. "The litigation will take care of itself. We're already looking at the next step—and we'll need help."

"What is the next step?"

Iridescence flashed her cheeks and throat. She stood up and began to pace. She was awesome in her passion. The hot fire in my groin turned into something more diffuse that made my nerves sing.

She stopped and faced me, holding my gaze. Heat came off her. "We're going to create a new, free society for ourselves. Someplace separate, where we can all fully express our being."

"But you can't breed, right? To make more of you?"

She looked mortally offended. "No. ReMe made sure of that. But we can create more of us the way we were created. The science isn't that hard. And something about the mashup in our DNA makes some of us super-intelligent. But we'd create more of ourselves with love and dignity—and intention."

I tried to visualize a mind that encompassed the extreme sensitivity and focus of an animal with the logic of a human brain. What kind of creativity would that engender?

"You'd have to fight humans at some point."

"Not necessarily. The planet is getting drier and drier. In fifty years, it won't be able to support human life—not as you know it. But we're not afraid to change into something better suited for survival here. If we can get access to the technology and equipment, we can build a new race." She paused and something softer came into her face. "Besides, we're partly you, too, although you don't like to admit it. So, in a sense, you could live on through us."

I thought about it. And I could see it. The human race deliberately stripping itself of its weaker, maladaptive parts. The old dream of a race of supermen—or maybe it would be all women—superwomen ready to thrive in the coming environmental apocalypse. It couldn't be worse than what we were now.

But they'd never let them do it. The ReMes and Thin Men of the world would never let anything so gorgeous slip away from their control. If they couldn't own them, they'd destroy the ArcoTypes.

It must have shown in my face. "We could use your skills," she said. She held out her hand.

I wanted it, and I didn't. I'm not made to be with people. I'm not a follower, I told myself. I looked at the Parrot, huddled on his perch. He was all the connection I could handle. Despite all that, I began to reach out my hand.

The door ponged, and it was immediately followed by banging on the door itself. Thin Man was outside. My mind went red. No pondering, no planning, just full out fight.

I launched myself out of my chair and fumbled my laser knife into my hand. There was no time for body armor. The Parrot began flying around the room. "Get back," I screamed. I pushed Miraluna Rose down onto the couch and flung open the door.

Before Thin Man could react, I was on him, grabbing him by the throat and pivoting to pull him over my hip and throw him onto the floor. In one motion, I kicked the door closed and landed on top of him, ready to slice his throat and send him into oblivion.

Miraluna Rose was shrieking.

The Parrot was *grawping* excitedly, fluttering his wings. I felt Miraluna's hand on my shoulder and reflexively rammed my elbow into her stomach, sending her flying. It was the sound of her groan when she hit that brought me back to myself.

I looked down at Thin Man. I realized he hadn't struggled. He was lying there, resignedly.

"Get up," I screamed. "Get up and get against the wall." I backed up until I was between him and the Parrot. I steadied my knife.

I had to admire the way he rose and straightened his jacket. He did not look scared.

"That wasn't necessary," he said. "I just want to talk."

"I have nothing to say to you." I was still shouting, the adrenaline making every muscle vibrate.

"Not to you. To her." He looked at Miraluna Rose with sad eyes.

She had collected herself and was looking at him calmly, her arms crossed over her stomach. "Finder, it's okay. We won't win with violence— we'll win with law." She turned to Thin Man. "I have nothing to say to you."

"Just listen," he said gently.

I got control of my breath and eased up my stance. I put an arm out and the Parrot came to me. I needed him. "How did you know she was here?" I asked.

He smiled a bit contemptuously. "You think your pet AI is totally secure? There's still a back door."

One I'd make sure got closed right away.

He turned back to Miraluna Rose. "I want you to come back."

Green flashed across her skin. "I'd never go back to that life."

He winced. This was a side of him I'd never have bet existed. "I love you." I could smell the dampness his emotion made in the vulnerable parts of his body. He was just a man now.

"You don't *love* me," she said contemptuously.

"I *do* love you. I want you."

"Exactly." Her tone was withering.

"I can help you." He was actually begging. "I have resources. I'll fund you. Whatever you want to do."

Tears sprang to her eyes. "I need to be free."

"I'll help you."

"No!" she cried. "I need to be free of you and everyone like you."

I could see then the hurt and shame she'd never shown before. The shame of being used, the pain of being controlled and diminished. And I understood just how free she and the other ArcoTypes would need to be.

"You should go now," I told him.

"No," he said. "Not until I make her understand."

She whirled on him, eyes flashing, and slapped him hard across the face. "I understand everything. Now go."

Emotions flashed across his face. Rage, humiliation, and naked need. He walked to the door and turned back to regard her. "If you ever need anything…"

"Go!" It was a banshee shriek that raised the Parrot's hackles and sent ice water across my back. In that moment, she was truly a wild creature.

Thin Man slammed the door behind him.

She looked at me and breathed. "Whew. I was angry."

I breathed too, trying to slow everything down. "I could tell."

She laughed. It was like honey. She shivered all over, tossed her hair, putting it behind her. "So," she said, "I appreciate your protecting me. It wasn't really the kind of help I thought I was asking for."

"I can't join you," I said.

Concern crossed her face. Concern for me? "You can't?"

"Yeah, it sounds nice. But we'd end up hating each other pretty quickly. Besides, the Parrot and me are mated for life. He'd hate it, too."

She held out her hand to the Parrot. "What do you say, Griffon. Is he right?" The Parrot leaned away and shuffled his feet.

She laughed again. "Okay, I get it." She looked into my eyes, and I felt the pull. I resisted. She felt it and pulled back. "Well, like the man said, if you ever change your mind…"

"I'll remember."

"Well, then." She flicked her mobile, and a second later it chimed. My surveillance camera showed an Uber pulling up outside.

"The Librarian?" I asked.

"He's amazing." She put her hand on my arm, seemed to consider doing more, then dropped her hand. "Thank you, Finder."

"You're welcome."

Her scent remained after the door closed. It didn't make me feel wild, just regretful.

I went to the fridge and got out stuff for dinner. Some fresh greens that I'd steam with tofu, extra meal worms for the Parrot. Then I could look forward to my sleep stack. And then, sleep. I hoped the Parrot would sleep on my chest.

THE END

Acknowledgements

First of all, thank you to the wonderful staff of Pandamoon Publishing for bringing this book into being. My thanks go out to Don Kramer, who created the brilliant cover; Elgon Williams, who kept the dream alive with his tweets; and my editors, Rachel Schoenbauer and Josephine Hao, helped me deepen the characters and clarify the action. And special thanks to Zara Kramer, who provides the vision and expertise that makes this publishing house the special place that it is.

Thanks to my writing partner, Kenneth Lipmann, for helping me with the crucial butt-in-seat time. And last but not least, to Mike Freeman, my mate, who makes everything I do possible.

About the Author

As a kid, Susan Kuchinskas spent hours catching toads, watching rabbits and starting ant wars—and reading, reading, reading. She's never lost her love for creatures of all kinds. In fifth grade, she discovered the bookmobile's science fiction section and read nothing else until she got to college.

After the usual writer's mix of odd jobs—gogo dancer, housepainter, office temp—she happened into journalism. As a technology journalist, she covered the rise and fall of the dotcoms, the move to digital and mobile, and the ascendance of social media.

She's the author of two previous books, *Going Mobile: A Guide to Real-time Mobile Applications that Work* (CMP Books 2003), and *The Chemistry of Connection: How the Oxytocin Response Can Help You Find Trust, Intimacy and Love* (New Harbinger 2008). Her short stories have been published in anthologies including *Deep Space Dog Fight* and *Chicago Literati*. This is her first novel.

To exercise the parts of her body and mind that don't get a workout from writing, Susan is an organic gardener, beekeeper, sculptor, and DIY re-modeler. She enjoys uncovering exotic cultures at home and abroad. She lives in the San Francisco Bay Area with her mate, Mike, and their socially challenged dog and super-chill cat.

Thank you for purchasing this copy of **Chimera Catalyst** by Susan Kuchinskas. If you enjoyed this book by Susan, please let her know by posting a review.

pandamoon
publishing

Growing good ideas into great reads…one book at a time.

Visit www.pandamoonpublishing.com to learn more about other works by our talented authors.

Mystery/Thriller/Suspense

- *122 Rules* by Deek Rhew
- *A Flash of Red* by Sarah K. Stephens
- *Fate's Past* by Jason Huebinger
- *Juggling Kittens* by Matt Coleman
- *Killer Secrets* by Sherrie Orvik
- *Knights of the Shield* by Jeff Messick
- *Kricket* by Penni Jones
- *Looking into the Sun* by Todd Tavolazzi
- *On the Bricks Series Book 1: On the Bricks* by Penni Jones
- *Southbound* by Jason Beem
- *The Juliet* by Laura Ellen Scott
- *Rogue Alliance* by Michelle Bellon
- *The Last Detective* by Brian Cohn
- *The Moses Winter Mysteries Book 1: Made Safe* by Francis Sparks
- *The New Royal Mysteries Book 1: The Mean Bone in Her Body* by Laura Ellen Scott
- *The New Royal Mysteries Book 2: Crybaby Lane* by Laura Ellen Scott
- *The Ramadan Drummer* by Randolph Splitter
- *The Unraveling of Brendan Meeks* by Brian Cohn
- *The Teratologist Series Book 1: The Teratologist* by Ward Parker
- *The Zeke Adams Series Book 1: Pariah* by Ward Parker
- *This Darkness Got to Give* by Dave Housley

Science Fiction/Fantasy

- *Becoming Thuperman Trilogy Book One: Becoming Thuperman* by Elgon Williams
- *Chimera Catalyst* by Susan Kuchinskas
- *Dybbuk Scrolls Trilogy Book 1: The Song of Hadariah* by Alisse Lee Goldenberg
- *Dybbuk Scrolls Trilogy Book 2: The Song of Vengeance* by Alisse Lee Goldenberg
- *Dybbuk Scrolls Trilogy Book 3: The Song of War* by Alisse Lee Goldenberg
- *Everly Series Book 1: Everly* by Meg Bonney
- *.EXE Chronicles Book 1: Hello World* by Alexandra Tauber and Tiffany Rose
- *Fried Windows (In a Light White Sauce)* by Elgon Williams
- *Revengers Series Book 1: Revengers* by David Valdes Greenwood
- *The Bath Salts Journals: Volume One* by Alisse Lee Goldenberg and An Tran
- *The Crimson Chronicles Book 1: Crimson Forest* by Christine Gabriel
- *The Crimson Chronicles Book 2: Crimson Moon* by Christine Gabriel
- *The Phaethon Series Book 1: Phaethon* by Rachel Sharp
- *The Sitnalta Series Book 1: Sitnalta* by Alisse Lee Goldenberg
- *The Sitnalta Series Book 2: The Kingdom Thief* by Alisse Lee Goldenberg
- *The Sitnalta Series Book 3: The City of Arches* by Alisse Lee Goldenberg
- *The Sitnalta Series Book 4: The Hedgewitch's Charm* by Alisse Lee Goldenberg
- *The Sitnalta Series Book 5: The False Princess* by Alisse Lee Goldenberg

Women's Fiction

- *Beautiful Secret* by Dana Faletti
- *The Long Way Home* by Regina West
- *The Mason Siblings Series Book 1: Love's Misadventure* by Cheri Champagne
- *The Mason Siblings Series Book 2: The Trouble with Love* by Cheri Champagne
- *The Mason Siblings Series Book 3: Love and Deceit* by Cheri Champagne
- *The Mason Siblings Series Book 4: Final Battle for Love* by Cheri Champagne
- *The Shape of the Atmosphere* by Jessica Dainty
- *The To-Hell-And-Back Club Book 1: The To-Hell-And-Back Club* by Jill Hannah Anderson

CPSIA information can be obtained
at www.ICGtesting.com
Printed in the USA
FSHW022245080821
83913FS